THE

Stephanie O. Abraham.

The Fire

Copyright: Stephanie O. Abraham

Published By: Book Writing Founders.

Unless otherwise indicated, all Scripture quotations in this book are from the King James Version of the Bible. Some Scripture quotations marked NIV are taken from the New International Version; NET quotations are taken from the New English Translation, while those marked AMP are from The Amplified Bible. Some illustrations are from Nelson's Illustrated Bible Dictionary.

All rights reserved. No portion of this book may be reproduced, stored in a retrieval system, or be transmitted in any form or by any means: mechanical, electronic, photocopying or otherwise without the prior written permission of the copyright owner. For further information, enquiries or permission, please write to:

Stephanie O. Abraham

Graphics and Cover Design: Stephanie O. Abraham and Prof. Iyiola Fawole

Printed in the United Kingdom.

E-mail: soabraham12@gmail.com

DEDICATION

This book is dedicated to my Creator, Lord and King, Master, Redeemer, Lover of my soul, my Friend and Eternal Father. "The Consuming Fire Himself" the Amen. Hallelujah!

ACKNOWLEDGEMENT

The writing of this book has been through divine inspiration and revelation. Over the years, I have been challenged with the first revelation the Lord opened my father's eyes to see the night he gave his life to the Lord Jesus Christ. His exact words were, "If you were not my daughter, I would not have believed it," among many words. Since then, I have been curious, searching for and believing in this opportunity to share this experience with brethren all around the world.

I am very deeply appreciative of the love, support, time, help and prompt advice that I received and enjoyed from my precious children. Despite the difficult challenges we have faced in our pilgrimage, the love, mercy, and grace of God have always been there to suffix us. His banner over us is truly love.

I also sincerely appreciate the support, corrections, comments and advice on actions concerning graphics and other important issues that I receive from my great Uncle regularly, from my mentors, various leaders and members of Harbour House Worldwide. Your sincere and meaningful words of encouragement that you gave at the appropriate time are well recorded in Heaven. The Lord will always bless you all. Amen.

Stephanie O. Abraham

Table of Contents

FOREWORD

The main purpose of this book is to try as much as possible to write in line with the Word of God, going deep into the Scriptures and finding out the real truth because deliverance lies in the truth. The more truth a man knows, the more his freedom shall be. The Truth that we as believers should cravingly desire to know is the Word of God, which is our Lord Jesus Christ. Fire is an interesting thing to examine. The sparkling, the glow and the generated heat, with the work or the result that comes out of its activities, makes it peculiar in its own special way. When God finished the work of creation in Genesis 1: 31, "God saw all that He had made, and it was very good" (NIV). The way we use fire is what is important and is the determinant factor of the kind of result that we will get. Whether it is the natural or the supernatural fire, the outcome depends on us.

God is illustrated as Fire. "Fire begat Fire," and so as children of God, we need to have deeper insight: For our "God is a consuming fire," as stated in Hebrews 12: 29 and Deuteronomy 4: 24. Imagine yourself as a believer walking in the consciousness of God who is inside us. He is the greater one that is in us than the one that is in the world. He is living on the inside of us. Within us, "our body" is the residence of God together with His Fire, anointing, power, glory, prosperity, ability and every other attribute and things that God have. Then He said He has made us, His servant, as Flames of Fire. This means the FIRE from within is flaming out on the surface, as flames either ignite or consume. Fire also purifies; according to Webster's dictionary, fire refines and makes free from impurities and imperfection. It is also the process used to purify precious metals like silver and gold. As the metals are heated up, the "dross" rises to the surface and is skimmed off. So also, we need to be purified by fire for heavenly effective assignments. You are a Fire, as our Father is "The Consuming Fire." Say to and remind yourself constantly. I AM A FIRE!

Praise God, Hallelujah! Amen.

CHAPTER ONE - WHAT IS FIRE?

Fire is the heat and light energy that is released during a chemical reaction, in particular, a combustion reaction. Combustion on its own means the process of burning. It is the state, condition or level of combustion producing heat, flames and smoke. Fire is the combustion of flammable materials. A flammable material is an article or substance that is easily set on fire. Three conditions must exist before a fire can be made. There must be a fuel or substance to burn. The fuel must be heated to its ignition temperature, the lowest temperature at which combustion can begin and be sustained. Finally, there must be plenty of oxygen, which usually comes from the surrounding air. Depending on the substances' alight and any impurities within, the colour of the flame and the fire intensity might vary.

Primitive people regarded fire as supernatural in origin and especially divine. The discovery of fire antedates history and seems to be assumed in the first sacrifice of Cain and

Abel in Genesis 4:3-4. No nation has yet been discovered that did not know the use of fire, but the way in which it was first procured is unknown. The ancient Greeks considered fire one of the major elements in the universe, alongside water, earth and air. This grouping makes intuitive sense: You can feel the fire, just like you can feel earth, water and air. You can also see it and smell it, and you can move it from place to place. But the fire is really something completely different. Earth, water and air are all forms of matter, and they are made up of millions and millions of atoms collected together. Fire is not a matter at all. It is a visible, tangible side effect of matter changing form, which is one part of a chemical reaction.

At least in later times, the Israelites seemed to have produced fire by striking steel against flint, even though the oldest method known was that of rubbing two pieces of wood or stones (pebbles) together. It could also be derived from the burning of coal or wood or a gas or electric device used in heating a room.[1] The dryness of the land in the hot season made fires more likely to occur, as written in Judges 9:15. The thorn bush said to the trees, "If you really want to choose me as your king, then come along, find safety under my branches! Otherwise may fire blaze from the thornbush and consume the cedars of Lebanon!" (NET). This usually could be a sudden, uncontrolled, and destructive fire from dryness of the leaves in the bush through extreme heat from the sunlight, from fire rampages occurring through unknown sources or from eruptions as in volcanic mountains.

The onset of fire could also come from the shooting of guns or another weapon that is being operated so that a bullet or missile is released. The law ordered that anyone kindling a fire that caused damage to grain should make restitution, according to Exodus 22:6; "If a fire breaks out and spreads to thorn bushes so that stacked grain or standing grain or the whole field is consumed, the one who started the fire must surely make restitution" —(NET).

As the outbreak of physical fire cannot be hidden, so is it with the spiritual fire in the spiritual realm. The outbreak of Holy Spirit Fire on a child of God cannot be hidden, nor can it be pushed back. It is extremely outstandingly glorious, extraordinarily admirable, illuminating, affecting, untouchable, purifying, consuming, and can be devastating and dangerous, and nothing can withstand the burning force. In the Bible, fire often appears as a symbol of God's presence

---

[1] Gowlett J. A. (2016). The discovery of fire by humans: a long and convoluted process. Philosophical transactions of the Royal Society of London. Series B, Biological sciences, 371(1696), 20150164. https://doi.org/10.1098/rstb.2015.0164

and power. The appearance of God's power comes with the feeling or sensation of heat from the anointing of the Holy Spirit.

In its first biblical use of this word, Fire represents God's presence in His covenant with Abraham as "a torch of fire" in Genesis 15:17- 18, saying, "When the sun had set, and darkness had fallen, a smoking brazier with a blazing torch appeared and passed between the pieces. On that day, the LORD made a covenant with Abram and said, 'To your descendants, I give this land, from the river of Egypt to the great river, the Euphrates.'" (NIV)

Fire's symbolism and significance extend beyond its religious, historical and practical aspects. It holds a unique place in the human psyche as a symbol of passion, inspiration and renewal. Fire has long been associated with the spark of creativity and innovation, as seen in idiomatic expressions like "the fire of invention" or "fiery passion." The mesmerising flames have captivated artists, writers and thinkers throughout history, inspiring creativity and igniting the human imagination. The element of fire embodies the very essence of change and transformation, often paralleling the human experience of growth and evolution.

In literature and mythology, fire is a recurring motif, often representing a source of knowledge, illumination and revelation. Similarly, in the modern era, the harnessing of fire's energy has been central to technological advancements. The industrial revolution was fueled by steam engines, which relied on controlled combustion, while electricity generation often involves harnessing the heat of fire to produce power. Even in the digital age, the term "firewall" is used to protect computer networks from unauthorised access, drawing a connection between fire's role as a barrier and its ancient function in protecting communities from external threats.

In summary, fire's significance goes far beyond its physical properties and historical uses. It is a symbol deeply embedded in human culture, representing not only the practical aspects of survival but also the spiritual, creative and transformative dimensions of the human experience.

Fire is fast. It is hot and very deadly. It is phenomenal.

CHAPTER TWO - ANCIENT USE AND BELIEF OF FIRE

The Israelites and other ancient cultures placed great value on fire. Entering so largely into the life of men, it has naturally been the subject of many legends. Fire and other forms of idol worshipping, having fire involvement, were practiced in many cultures of the ancient world, including the Medes, the Persians and the Canaanites. In an effort to appease their gods, the Canaanites even sacrificed their children on flaming altars.[2] Molech, the fire god, and other deities were worshipped by certain Canaanitish and other tribes with human sacrifices. The ancient Chaldeans regarded Gibir (or Gibil), the lord of fire, as their most powerful auxiliary against the Annunaki, an order of inferior but malicious beings. Gibir is addressed as the one who lightens up the darkness, who melts the copper and tin, the gold and silver. According to Greek mythology, Prometheus, when Zeus denied fire to mortals, stole it from Olympus and brought it to men in a hollow reed. For this, he was punished by being chained to a rock in the wilds of Scythia.

The Israelites, particularly, thought of fire as a symbol of God's mystical presence as well as His power and Judgement. In Deuteronomy 12: 31 it is written, "Thou shalt not do so unto the LORD thy God: for every abomination to

---

[2] Henry. (2013). Canaanite Child Sacrifice, Abortion, and the Bible, Journal of Ministry and Theology, Summit University, pp 90-125, https://www.academia.edu/28849418/Canaanite_Child_Sacrifice_Abor tion_and_the_Bible

the LORD, which he hateth, have they done unto their gods; for even their sons and their daughters they have burnt in the fire to their gods;" of this such abomination stated in Ezekiel 16:20-21 "You took your sons and your daughters whom you bore to me and you sacrificed them as food for the idols to eat. As if your prostitution not enough, you slaughtered my children and sacrificed them to the idols;" 2 Kings 16:3; He followed in the footsteps of the kings of Israel. He passed his son through the fire, a horrible sin practiced by the nations whom the LORD drove out from before the Israelites, and 2 Chronicles 28: 3; He offered sacrifices in the Valley of Ben-Hinnom and passed his sons through the fire, a horrible sin practiced by the nations whom the LORD drove out before the Israelites (NET).

God often warned Israel that this practice was an abomination to Him and that they should not participate in their neighbours' sin. Although this was specially forbidden to the Israelites, they too often lapsed into the practice. Up to this day and age, in many parts of the world, this kind of similar belief and idol way of worshipping or activity still exists, where sacrifices are being made by fire in many cultural sections or groups. In Africa, "Sango" – a man possessed by a demon was believed to be the god of thunder who brings out fire from its mouth to consume its enemies when in wrath towards them and operates mainly with heavy rainfall, lightning, and thunder. Fire was used to consume the burnt offerings and the incense offerings. This began with the sacrifice of Noah in Genesis 8:20-21 as written; "Noah built an altar to the LORD. He then took some of every kind of clean animal and clean bird and offered burnt offerings on the altar. And the LORD smelled the soothing aroma and said to himself, 'I will never again curse the ground because of humankind, even though the inclination of their minds is evil from childhood on. I will never again destroy everything that lives, as I have just done.'" (NET) and continuing in the ever-burning fire on the altar as in Leviticus 6: 9, saying, "Command Aaron and his sons, "This is the law of the burnt offering. The burnt offering is to remain on the hearth on the altar all night until morning, and the fire of the altar must be kept burning on it" (NET).

In the sacrificial flame, the essence of the animal was resolved into vapour; so that when a man presented a sacrifice in his own stead, his innermost being, his spirit, and his heart ascended to God in the vapour, and the sacrifice brought the feeling of his heart before God.

This altar fire was sometimes miraculously sent from God like the fire from the Lord that consumed the sacrifices of David according to 1 Chronicles 21:26; "David built there an altar to the LORD and offered burnt sacrifices and peace offerings. He called out to the LORD, and the LORD responded by sending fire from the sky and consuming the burnt sacrifice on the altar," and with Solomon respectively in 2 Chronicles 7:1; "When Solomon finished praying, fire came down from heaven and consumed the burnt offering and the sacrifices, and the LORD's splendour filled the temple" (NET).

On God's instructions in the Old Testament, fire was to be constantly burning upon the altar without going out. In order that the burnt offering might never go out because this was the divinely appointed symbol and visible sign of the uninterrupted worship of God Almighty, which the covenant nation could never suspend either day or night without being unfaithful to its calling according to Leviticus 6:12-13, "but the fire which is on the altar must be kept burning on it. It must not be extinguished. So the priest must kindle wood on it morning by morning, and he must arrange the burnt offering on it and offer the fat of the peace offering up in smoke on it. A continual fire must be kept burning on the altar. It must not be extinguished" (NET).

Fire for sacred purposes obtained elsewhere apart from the altar was called "strange fire," for the use of which Nadab and Abihu were punished with death by fire from God; according to Leviticus 10:1-2, "Then Aaron's sons, Nadab and Abihu, each took his fire pan and put fire in it, set incense on it, and presented strange fire before the LORD, which he had not commanded them to do. So fire went out from the presence of the LORD and consumed them so that they died before the LORD," confirmed in Numbers 3:4, saying, "Nadab and Abihu died before the LORD when they offered strange fire before the LORD in the wilderness of

Sinai, and they had no children. So Eleazar and Ithamar ministered as priests in the presence of Aaron, their father" and also in Numbers 26:61, "But Nadab and Abihu died when they offered strange fire before the LORD" (NET).

When the Israelites returned with booty taken from the Midianites, Eleazer whose duty was to see that the laws of purification were properly observed, told them that "the statute of the law" was that all the articles that could bear the fire, were to be drawn through it, and then sprinkled with the water of purification while the animals slain for sin offerings were afterward consumed by fire outside of the camp according to Leviticus 4:12, "Even the whole bullock shall he carry forth without the camp unto a clean place, where the ashes are poured out, and burn him on the wood with fire: where the ashes are poured out shall he be burnt" and verse 21 stated, "And he shall carry forth the bullock without the camp, and burn him as he burned the first bullock: it is a sin offering for the congregation," while Leviticus 6:30 said, "And no sin offering, whereof any of the blood is brought into the tabernacle of the congregation to reconcile withal in the holy place, shall be eaten: it shall be burnt in the fire," and Leviticus 16:27 stated, "And the bullock for the sin offering, and the goat for the sin offering, whose blood was brought in to make atonement in the holy place, shall one carry forth without the camp; and they shall burn in the fire their skins, and their flesh, and their dung," and Hebrews 13:11 confirmed it saying; "For the bodies of those beasts, whose blood is brought into the sanctuary by the high priest for sin, are burned without the camp."

A Nazarite, on the day when the time of his consecration expired, must shave his head and put the hair into the altar fire under the peace offering that was burning, thus handing over and sacrificing to the Lord the hair that had been worn in honour of Him such as it is written in Numbers 6:18, "And the Nazarite shall shave the head of his separation at the door of the tabernacle of the congregation, and shall take the hair of the head of his separation, and put it in the fire which is under the sacrifice of the peace offerings."

In the Old Testament, fire and flame were closely associated with Israel's worship and religious life. God also used fire to guide His people, and God spoke to Moses in the burning bush experience and called him to lead the children of Israel out of the Egyptian bondage according to Exodus 3:2-12, "And the angel of the LORD appeared unto him in a flame of fire out of the midst of a bush: and he looked, and, behold, the bush burned with fire, and the bush was not consumed. And Moses said, I will now turn aside, and see this great sight, why the bush is not burnt. And when the LORD saw that he turned aside to see, God called unto him out of the midst of the bush, and said, Moses, Moses. And he said, Here am I. And he said, Draw not nigh hither: put off thy shoes from off thy feet, for the place whereon thou standest is holy ground. Moreover, he said, I am the God of thy father, the God of Abraham, the God of Isaac, and the God of Jacob. And Moses hid his face, for he was afraid to look upon God. And the LORD said I have surely seen the affliction of my people which are in Egypt, and have heard their cry by reason of their taskmasters; for I know their sorrows; And I am come down to deliver them out of the hand of the Egyptians, and to bring them up out of that land unto a good land flowing with milk and honey; unto the place of the Canaanites, and the Hittites, and the Amorites, and the Perizzites, and the Hivites, and the Jebusites. Now therefore, behold, the cry of the children of Israel is come unto me: and I have also seen the oppression wherewith the Egyptians oppress them. Come now, therefore, and I will send thee unto Pharaoh, that thou mayest bring forth my people, the children of Israel, out of Egypt. And Moses said unto God, Who am I, that I should go unto Pharaoh, and that I should bring forth the children of Israel out of Egypt? And he said, Certainly I will be with thee, and this shall be a token unto thee, that I have sent thee: When thou hast brought forth the people out of Egypt, ye shall serve God upon this mountain."

The other various uses of fire are given according to these categories and are still in use today in the same way all over the world, such as the Physical, Domestic and Supernatural uses.

The Physical uses:

Metalwork: The use of charcoal in reducing and fashioning metals was well known among the Hebrews, Palestine and generally all over the world even till today. They used it to forge their tools and weapons. These tools and weapons are instruments that are particularly used for battles and also their daily living activities like farming, ploughing, hunting for games or any other kind of metalwork needed for the construction of buildings and roads.

The Domestic uses.

Cooking and Warmth*:* The preparation of food presupposes the use of fire. Besides for cooking purposes, fire is often needed for warmth in winter, as stated in Jeremiah 36:22, "Now the king sat in the winter house in the ninth month: and there was a fire on the hearth burning before him," also in Mark 14:54 saying, "And Peter followed him afar off, even into the palace of the high priest: and he sat with the servants, and warmed himself at the fire," and in John 18:18: "And the servants and officers stood there, who had made a fire of coals; for it was cold: and they warmed themselves: and Peter stood with them, and warmed himself."

Sometimes, a hearth with a chimney was constructed, on which lighted wood or a pan of charcoal was placed. In Persia, a hole made in the floor is sometimes filled with charcoal, on which a sort of table is set and covered with a carpet, and the company draws the carpet over their feet for warmth. Rooms are also warmed in Egypt with pans of charcoal.

The laws regulating Fire include the law forbidding any fire to be kindled on the Sabbath, even for culinary purposes, such as in Exodus 35:3, "You must not kindle a fire in any of your homes on the Sabbath day," and in Numbers 15:32-36, "When the Israelites were in the wilderness they found a man gathering wood on the Sabbath day. Those who found him gathering wood brought him to Moses and Aaron and to the whole community. They put him in custody because there was no clear instruction about what should be done to him. Then the LORD said to Moses, 'The man must surely be put to death; the whole community must stone him with stones outside the camp,' So the whole community took him outside the camp and stoned him to death, just as the LORD commanded Moses" (NET).

Signs: Judges 20:38 and 40 says, "Now there was an appointed sign between the men of Israel and the liers in wait, that they should make a great flame with smoke rise up out of the city. But when the flame began to arise up out of the city with a pillar of smoke, the Benjamites looked behind them, and, behold, the flame of the city ascended up to heaven." There was a conflict between the Israelites and the Benjamites. The Israelites devised a plan to attack the city where the Benjamites were hiding. They had a secret signal to coordinate their attack. The signal involved creating a large flame with smoke rising from the city. This was a predetermined sign agreed upon by the Israelite forces and the group of men lying in ambush.

When the appointed time came, and the Israelites set the city on fire, a great flame and pillar of smoke rose up from the city. This was the signal to the Israelite forces to begin their attack. However, in verse 40, it says that the Benjamites, who were the defenders of the city, saw the flame and smoke rising so high that it appeared to reach up to heaven. This likely means that the fire and smoke were extremely conspicuous, indicating that the attack had begun.

Torture: Daniel 3:6 says, "And whoso falleth not down and worshippeth shall the same hour be cast into the midst of a burning fiery furnace." King Nebuchadnezzar of Babylon erected a large golden statue and commanded all the people in his kingdom to bow down and worship it when they heard music playing. The consequence for not obeying this command was severe, as mentioned in Daniel 3:6. It states that anyone who did not fall down and worship the golden statue when they heard the music would be cast into the midst of a burning fiery furnace.

The idea here is that those who refused to worship the statue would face torture through being thrown into a furnace where they would be burnt alive. This was a form of punishment used to enforce the king's authority and the state religion. The story goes on to describe how three Jewish men named Shadrach, Meshach and Abednego refused to bow down to the statue, even though they knew the consequences. As a result, they were indeed thrown into the fiery furnace but miraculously survived, unharmed, through divine intervention.

Penal: Capital punishment was sometimes aggravated by burning the body of the criminal after death as written in

Leviticus 20:14, "And if a man take a wife and her mother, it is wickedness: they shall be burnt with fire, both he and they; that there be no wickedness among you," while Leviticus 21: 9 stated that the daughter of any priest who profanes herself by playing the harlot profanes her father; she shall be burned with fire [after being stoned] (AMP). This is serious. Now we have the grace of God; why should it be taken for granted? Lord have mercy!

In Joshua 7:25, it is written, "And Joshua said, Why hast thou troubled us? The LORD shall trouble thee this day. And all Israel stoned him with stones, and burned them with fire after they had stoned them with stones and according to 2 Kings 23:16; it says, "And as Josiah turned himself, he spied the sepulchres that were there in the mount, and sent, and took the bones out of the sepulchres, and burned them upon the altar, and polluted it, according to the word of the LORD which the man of God proclaimed, who proclaimed these words."

The Supernatural uses:

Sacrifices: Genesis 8:20- 21 says that Noah built an altar unto the LORD; and took of every clean beast, and of every clean fowl, and offered burnt offerings on the altar. "And the LORD smelled a sweet savour; and the LORD said in his heart, I will not again curse the ground any more for man's sake; for the imagination of man's heart is evil from his youth; neither will I again smite any more everything living, as I have done."

Refining: While in refining, Psalms 12:6 declares that the words of the LORD are pure words: as silver tried in a furnace of earth, purified seven times.

Testing of Works: In 1 Corinthians 3:12-15, fire is used to test the quality of a person's work: "If anyone builds on this foundation using gold, silver, costly stones, wood, hay or straw, their work will be shown for what it is, because the Day will bring it to light. It will be revealed with fire, and the fire will test the quality of each person's work."

Manifest God: In Exodus 3:2, it is written that the angel of the LORD appeared unto him in a flame of fire out of the midst of a bush: and he looked, and beholds, the bush burned with fire, and the bush was not consumed.

Indicate God's power: Also, in Exodus 9:24, it is written, "So there was hail; and fire mingled with the hail, very grievous, such as there was none like it in all the land of Egypt since it became a nation."

Express God's approval: While in Leviticus 9:24, it is written there came a fire out from before the LORD, and consumed upon the altar the burnt offering and the fat: which when all the people saw, they shouted, and fell on their faces.

Vindicate God's wrath: "Then the king sent unto him a captain of fifty with his fifty. And he went up to him: and, behold, he sat on the top of a hill. And he spake unto him, Thou man of God, the king hath said, Come down. And Elijah answered and said to the captain of fifty, if I be a man of God, then let fire come down from heaven, and consume thee and thy fifty. And there came down fire from heaven and consumed him and his fifty. Again also he sent unto him another captain of fifty with his fifty. And he answered and said unto him, O man of God, thus hath the king said, come down quickly. And Elijah answered and said unto them, if I be a man of God, let fire come down from heaven, and consumes thee and thy fifty. And the fire of God came down from heaven, and consumed him and his fifty," according to 2 Kings 1:9- 12

Moreover, in the book of Revelation, the "lake of fire" is described as the final destination for the wicked and the devil. It's a symbol of eternal punishment and separation from God.

Guide Israel: "And the LORD went before them by day in a pillar of a cloud, to lead them the way; and by night in a pillar of fire, to give them light; to go by day and night: He took not away the pillar of the cloud by day, nor the pillar of fire by night, from before the people," declares Exodus 13:21-22.

Transport a saint to heaven: "And it came to pass, as they still went on, and talked, that, behold, there appeared a chariot of fire, and horses of fire, and parted them both asunder; and Elijah went up by a whirlwind into heaven," says 2 Kings 2:11.

Figuratively, fire was a symbol of the Lord's presence and the instrument of His power, either in the way of approval or of destruction such as in Exodus 14:19 and 24: "And the angel of God, which went before the camp of Israel, removed and went behind them; and the pillar of the cloud went from before their face, and stood behind them: And it came to pass, that in the morning watch the LORD looked unto the host of the Egyptians through the pillar of fire and of the cloud, and troubled the host of the Egyptians," and in Numbers 11:1 and 3; "And when the people complained, it displeased the LORD: and the LORD heard it; and his anger was kindled; and the fire of the LORD burnt among them, and consumed them that were in the uttermost parts of the camp, And he called the name of the place Taberah: because the fire of the LORD burnt among them," or even as in God appeared in the burning bush in Exodus 3:2 as written: "And the angel of the LORD appeared unto him in a flame of fire out of the midst of a bush: and he looked, and, behold, the bush burned with fire, and the bush was not consumed" and also on Mt. Sinai in Exodus 19:18, "And mount Sinai was altogether on a smoke, because the LORD descended upon it in fire: and the smoke thereof ascended as the smoke of a furnace, and the whole mount quaked greatly."

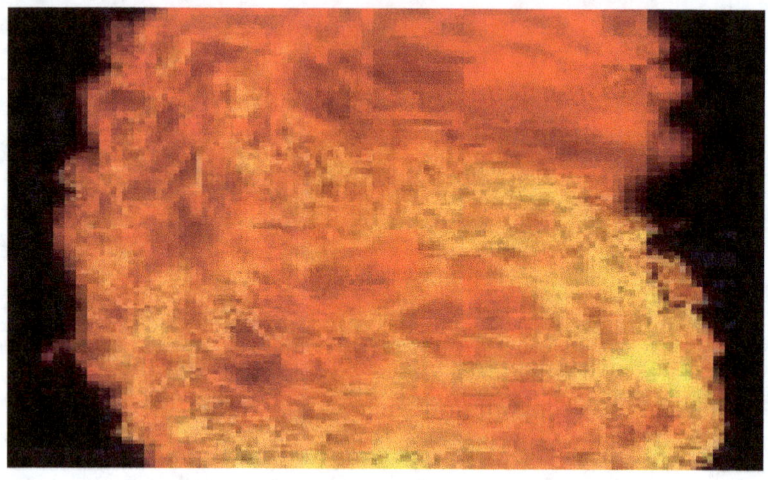

As God in Exodus 13:21 guided the Israelites through the wilderness with the pillar of fire, so also did He reveal Himself in the midst of fire to Isaiah, Ezekiel, and John according to Isaiah 6:4-5, "And the posts of the door moved at the voice of him that cried, and the house was filled with smoke. Then said I, Woe is me! for I am undone; because I am a man of unclean lips, and I dwell in the midst of a people of unclean lips: for mine eyes have seen the King, the LORD of hosts," and written in Ezekiel 1:4-5, "And I looked, and, behold, a whirlwind came out of the north, a great cloud, and a fire infolding itself, and a brightness was about it, and out of the midst thereof as the colour of amber, out of the midst of the fire. Also, out of the midst thereof came the likeness of four living creatures. And this was their appearance; they had the likeness of a man," and Revelation 1:12-14 says, "And I turned to see the voice that spake with me. And being turned, I saw seven golden candlesticks; And in the midst of the seven candlesticks one like unto the Son of man, clothed with a garment down to the foot, and girt about the paps with a golden girdle. His head and his hairs were white like wool, as white as snow, and his eyes were as a flame of fire." And in the same manner, He will so appear at His Second Coming as written in 2 Thessalonians 1:7-8 saying, "And to you who are troubled rest with us, when the Lord Jesus shall be revealed from heaven with his mighty angels, In flaming fire taking vengeance on them that know not God, and that obey not the gospel of our Lord Jesus Christ."

Fire is also used in the illustration of many things, such as in lust according to Proverbs 6:25-29, advising, Lust not after her beauty in thine heart; neither let her take thee with her eyelids. For by means of a whorish woman, a man is brought to a piece of bread: and the adulteress will hunt for the precious life. Can a man take fire in his bosom, and his clothes not be burned? Can one go upon hot coals and his feet not be burned? So he that goeth into his neighbour's wife; whosoever toucheth her shall not be innocent. While wickedness is illustrated in Isaiah 9:18, stating; For wickedness burneth as the fire: it shall devour the briers and thorns and shall kindle in the thickets of the forest, and they shall mount up like the lifting up of smoke. Also, in the tongue in Proverbs 16:27 declares; An ungodly man diggeth up evil: and in his lips there is as a burning fire and James 3:6 specifically said; And the tongue is a fire, a world of iniquity: so is the tongue among our members, that it defileth the whole body, and setteth on fire the course of nature; and it is set on fire of hell.

Isaiah 50:11 describes the hope of hypocrites, saying behold, all ye that kindle a fire that compass yourselves about with sparks: walk in the light of your fire, and in the sparks that ye have kindled. This shall ye have of mine hand; ye shall lie down in sorrow.

In regards to persecution, Luke 12:49-53 declared; I have come to send fire on the earth; and what will I, if it be already kindled? But I have a baptism to be baptised with, and how am I straitened till it be accomplished! Suppose ye that I am come to give peace on earth? I tell you, nay; but rather division: For from henceforth there shall be five in one house divided, three against two, and two against three. The father shall be divided against the son, and the son against the father; the mother against the daughter, and the daughter against the mother; the mother-in-law against her daughter-in-law, and the daughter-in-law against her mother-in-law. While of Judgement, Jeremiah 48:45 says; they that fled stood under the shadow of Heshbon because of the force: but a fire shall come forth out of Heshbon, and a flame from the midst of Sihon, and shall devour the corner of Moab, and the crown of the head of the tumultuous ones. Lamentation 1:13 also wrote; From above hath he sent fire into my bones, and it prevaileth against them: he hath spread a net for my feet, he hath turned me back: he hath made me desolate and faint all the day, and Ezekiel 39:6 says, And I will send a fire on Magog, and among them that dwell carelessly in the isles: and they shall know that I am the LORD. Amen.

CHAPTER THREE - FIRE PURIFICATION

First and foremost, in order to get a proper understanding of what FIRE PURIFICATION really is, it will be wise for us to know what PURITY and PURIFICATION are according to the Scriptures. So before I continue, we will be learning more about this aspect of our Christian character from the real source, 'The Bible.'

Purity - The quality or state of being free from mixture, pollution, contamination or other foreign elements.[3] The term purity may refer to things like Gold as written in Exodus 25:17: "And thou shalt make a mercy seat of pure gold: two cubits, and a half shall be the length thereof, and a cubit and a half the breadth thereof;" Oil in Leviticus 24:2; "Command the children of Israel, that they bring unto thee pure oil olive beaten for the light, to cause the lamps to burn continually." People's purity with reference to race as in Philippians 3:5; "Circumcised the eighth day, of the stock of Israel, of the tribe of Benjamin, a Hebrew of the Hebrews; as touching the law, a Pharisee;" and ceremonially according to Leviticus 19:16-33 which stated that "Never gossip. Never endanger your neighbor's life. I am the Lord. Never hate another Israelite. Be sure to correct your neighbor so that you will not be guilty of sinning along with him. Never get revenge. Never hold a grudge against any of your people. Instead, love your neighbor as you love yourself. I am the

---

[3] The Britannica Dictionary,
<https://www.britannica.com/dictionary/purity>

Lord. Obey my laws. Never crossbreed different kinds of animals. Never plant two kinds of crops in your field. Never wear clothes made from two kinds of material. If a man has sexual intercourse with a female slave who is engaged to another man and if her freedom was never bought or given to her, they should not be put to death. He will only pay a fine because she is a slave. He must bring a ram for his guilt offering to the Lord at the entrance to the tent of meeting. In the Lord's presence, the priest will use them to make peace with the Lord for this sin. The man will be forgiven for this sin. When you come into the land and plant all kinds of fruit trees, you must not eat the fruit for {the first} three years. In the fourth year, all the fruit will be a holy offering of praise to the Lord. In the fifth year, you may eat the fruit. Do this to make the trees produce more for you. I am the Lord your God. Never eat any meat with blood still in it. Never cast evil spells, and never consult fortune tellers. Never shave the hair on your foreheads, and never cut the edges of your beard. Never slash your body to mourn the dead, and never get a tattoo. I am the Lord. Never dishonor your daughter by making her a prostitute, or the country will turn to prostitution and be filled with people who are perverted. Observe my days of worship and respect my holy tent. I am the Lord. Don't turn to psychics or mediums to get help. That will make you unclean. I am the Lord your God. Show respect to the elderly and honor older people. In this way, you show respect for your God. I am the Lord. Never mistreat a foreigner living in your land (God's Word)."

Purity is not only a matter of physical substances but extends to human conduct and morality. The concept of purity in Leviticus 19:16-33 emphasises the importance of ethical and compassionate behaviour. This scriptural passage guides various aspects of interpersonal relationships, underlining the significance of maintaining a pure heart and good character. By avoiding actions such as gossip, hatred, revenge, and mistreatment of others, individuals can strive for moral purity. The notion of moral purity is central to many religious and philosophical traditions, highlighting the timeless value of integrity and kindness.

The idea of purity in the context of Leviticus also carries implications for societal harmony and justice. Beyond individual actions, these guidelines promote fairness and equity within the community. By showing respect to the elderly, honouring older people, and not mistreating foreigners living in the land, a sense of purity in community relationships is fostered. This concept reminds us that purity is an individual pursuit and a collective one, emphasising the importance of mutual respect and inclusivity within a society to create a pure and harmonious environment.

Ethically, in Luke 2:22 and Proverbs 22:11, while Spiritually in 1 Timothy 1:5 and 1 Timothy 4:12, The Jews of Jesus' day often took ceremonial purity beyond what Scripture commanded. They considered ceremonial purity more valuable than spiritual purity. Mark 7:3-4 said that "the Pharisees, and all the Jews, except they wash their hands oft, eat not, holding the tradition of the elders. And when they come from the market, except they wash, they do not eat. And many other things there are, which they have received to hold, as the washing of cups, and pots, brazen vessels, and of tables."

Luke11:39-41 declared, "And the Lord said unto him, Now do ye Pharisees make clean the outside of the cup and the platter; but your inward part is full of ravening and wickedness. Ye fools, did not he that made that which is without make that which is within also? But rather give alms of such things as ye have; and, behold, all things are clean unto you." For this error, Jesus soundly rebuked them in Mark 7:1-13. The purity which a Christian should strive for is spiritual in nature, unlike that of the Old Testament time, and that is the reason why Jesus rebuked them for their lack of insight in the above passage as well as in Luke 11: 39-41, Matthew 5:8 and James 1:27 respectively saying pure religion and undefiled before God and the Father is this, To visit the fatherless and widows in their affliction, and to keep himself unspotted from the world.

Purification - This is the act of making oneself clean and pure before God and men.[4] This act of purification involved religious and spiritual cleansing. Isaiah 6: 5-7 says, "Then said I, Woe is me! for I am undone; because I am a man of unclean lips, and I dwell in the midst of a people of unclean lips: for mine eyes have seen the King, the LORD of hosts. Then flew one of the Seraphims unto me, having a live coal in his hand, which he had taken with the tongs from off the altar: And he laid it upon my mouth, and said, Lo, this hath touched thy lips; and thine iniquity is taken away, and thy sin purged."

The Mosaic Law given by God to the Israelites then provided instructions for both physical and spiritual

---

[4] purification,
<https://dictionary.cambridge.org/dictionary/english/purification>

purification. These laws and regulations were much more than sanitary instructions. These Laws recognised and detailed purification rituals under three distinct categories of uncleanness. These were leprosy, Sexual discharges, and contact with a dead body. In Leviticus 13:1, Leviticus 14:1 and Leviticus 15:1, respectively, it state that "And the LORD spake unto Moses and Aaron, saying" and "He that toucheth the dead body of any man shall be unclean seven days. He shall purify himself with it on the third day, and on the seventh day, he shall be clean: but if he purify not himself the third day, then the seventh day, he shall not be clean. Whosoever toucheth the dead body of any man that is dead, and purifieth not himself, defileth the tabernacle of the LORD; and that soul shall be cut off from Israel: because the water of separation was not sprinkled upon him, he shall be unclean; his uncleanness is yet upon him. This is the law, when a man dieth in a tent: all that come into the tent, and all that is in the tent, shall be unclean seven days. And every open vessel, which hath no covering bound upon it, is unclean. And whosoever toucheth one that is slain with a sword in the open fields, or a dead body, or a bone of a man, or a grave, shall be unclean seven days. And for an unclean person they shall take of the ashes of the burnt heifer of purification for sin, and running water shall be put thereto in a vessel: And a clean person shall take hyssop, and dip it in the water, and sprinkle it upon the tent, and upon all the vessels, and upon the persons that were there, and upon him that touched a bone, or one slain, or one dead, or a grave: And the clean person shall sprinkle upon the unclean on the third day, and on the seventh day: and on the seventh day he shall purify himself, and wash his clothes, and bathe himself in water, and shall be clean at even," according to Numbers 19:11-19. By the time of Jesus, much had been added to the laws of purification, making them a burden to the people. Jesus denounced such rituals, teaching that defilement and uncleanness came from within or the inner motives of the mind and heart. He taught that genuine purification is possible only by following Him and giving heed to His message of love and redemption, as stated in Mark 7:14-23 and John 15:3, respectively. As written in Mark 7:14-23 NKJV, When He had called all the multitude to *Himself,* He said to them, "Hear Me, everyone, and understand: There is nothing that enters a man from outside which can defile him; but the things which come out of him, those are the things that defile a man. If anyone has ears to hear, let him hear!" When He had entered a house away from the crowd, His disciples asked Him concerning the parable. So He said to them, "Are you thus without understanding also? Do you not perceive that whatever enters a man from outside cannot defile him because it does not enter his heart but his stomach and is eliminated, thus purifying all foods?" And He said, "What comes out of a man, that defiles a man. For from within, out of the heart of men, proceed evil thoughts, adulteries, fornications, murders, thefts, covetousness, wickedness, deceit, lewdness, an evil eye, blasphemy, pride, foolishness. All these evil things come from within and defile a man," respectively, as written in John 15:3 NKJV, You are already clean because of the word which I have spoken to you.

The enduring relevance of Jesus' teachings on purity extends far beyond his historical era. His emphasis on inner purity remains a timeless guiding principle in a world marked by diverse religious and philosophical beliefs. It calls upon individuals to examine their own intentions, thoughts, and actions, fostering an enduring quest for spiritual growth. The idea that true purity comes from within has resonated with countless individuals seeking a deeper connection with their spirituality and a more profound understanding of themselves, echoing the profound impact of Jesus' message on purity throughout human history.

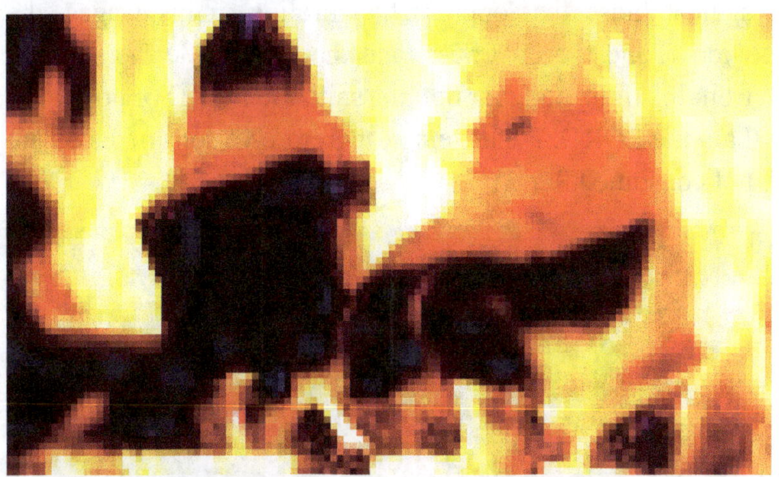

FIRE PURIFICATION:

As a source of heat and light, fire is often pictured in the Bible as God's agent to purify and illuminate. The coming Messenger of the Lord is portrayed as a "refiner's fire. In Malachi 3:1- 6, it says, "Behold, I will send my messenger, and he shall prepare the way before me: and the Lord, whom ye seek, shall suddenly come to his temple, even the messenger of the covenant, whom ye delight in: behold, he shall come, saith the LORD of hosts. But who may abide the day of his coming? And who shall stand when he appeareth? for he is like a refiner's fire, and like fullers' soap: And he shall sit as a refiner and purifier of silver: and he shall purify the sons, and he shall purify the sons of Levi, and purge them as gold and silver, that they may offer unto the LORD an offering in righteousness. Then shall the offering of Judah and Jerusalem be pleasant unto the LORD, as in the days of old, and as in former years. And I will come near to you to judgment, and I will be a swift witness against the sorcerers, and against the adulterers, and against false swearers, and against those that oppress the hireling in his wages, the widow, and the fatherless, and that turn aside the stranger from his right, and fear not me, saith the LORD of hosts. For I am the LORD, I change not; therefore ye sons of Jacob are not consumed."

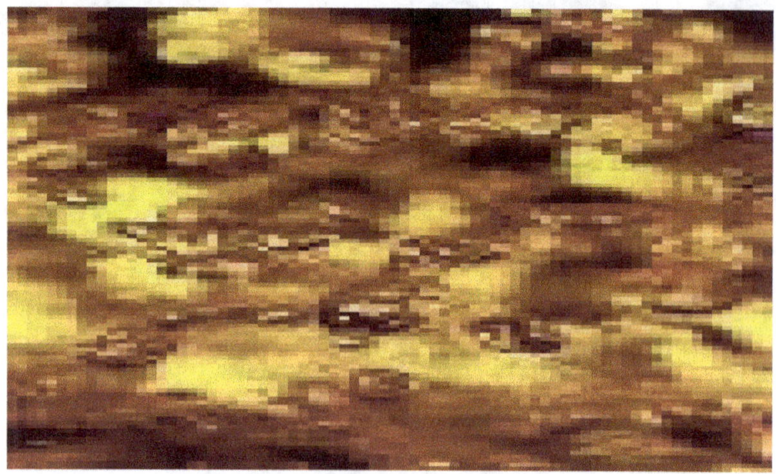

The purifying ability of the Fire of God adequately prepares His servants effectively for whatever task or ministerial job He has purposed for them to do. The tongues of fire, which came with the descent of the Holy Spirit at Pentecost, underscored the purging and illuminating quality of God's truth. Equipping and enabling them for the supernatural. Acts 2:1- 4: "And when the day of Pentecost was fully come, they were all with one accord in one place. And suddenly, there came a sound from heaven as of a rushing mighty wind, and it filled all the house where they were sitting. And there appeared unto them cloven tongues like as of fire, and it sat upon each of them. And they were all filled with the Holy Ghost, and began to speak with other tongues, as the Spirit gave them utterance."

We realise that in most cases and situations in the Bible when God calls His chosen ones for a divine task, there is always an accompaniment or significance of fire or oil involvement. According to the description which John gave of our Lord Jesus Christ in the book Revelation, we can see our perfect example who is Jesus, being described in relation to this in Revelation 1:11–20: "Saying, I am the Alpha and Omega, the first and the last: Write promptly what you see, (your vision) in a book and send it to the seven churches which are in Asia; to Ephesus and to Smyrna and to Pergamum and to Thyatira and to Sardis and to Philadelphia and to Laodicea. Then I turned to see (whose was) the voice that was speaking to me, and on turning, I saw seven golden lampstands. And in the midst of the lampstands (One) like a Son of man, clothed with a robe which reached to His feet and with a girdle of gold about His breasts. His head and His hair were white like white wool (as white) as snow, and His eyes (flashed) like a flame of fire. His feet glowed like burnished (bright) bronze as it is refined in a furnace, and His voice was like the sound of many waters. In His right hand, He held seven stars, and from His mouth, there came forth a sharp two-edged sword, and His face was like the sun shining in full power at midday. When I saw Him, I fell at

His feet as if dead. But He laid His right hand on me and said, Do not be afraid! I am the first and the last, And the Ever-living One (I am living in the eternity of the eternities). I died, but see, I am alive forevermore, and I possess the keys of death and of hades (the realm of the dead). Write, therefore, the things you see, what they are (and signify), and what is to take place hereafter. As to the hidden meaning (the mystery) of the seven stars which you saw on My right hand and the seven lampstands of gold: the seven stars are the seven angels (messengers) of the seven assemblies (churches), and the seven lampstands are the seven churches." (AMP)

This powerful description not only highlights the majestic nature of Christ but also underscores the connection between divine tasks and the symbols of fire and light, which are primary to the spiritual journey of believers. The purity, authority and anointing represented in this passage remind us of the sacred relationship between God and His chosen ones throughout history.

Examining the time and the instances or the happenings when some Prophets in the Bible were called and using their situations to explain or to compare with what our circumstances now should entail even at this time of the marvellous move of the Holy Spirit. Taking these prophets in the Bible as examples, from when they were called and the specifications of their call, a Prophet like Moses, who was called out of a burning bush, was a deliverer of the Israelites at that particular time. In which it has earlier been written over. So do we now, as God-chosen ones, need to realise how much we need to be purified by fire, which is an indication or the significance of a divine appointment, special honour, a special privilege, and God's blessing coupled with effectiveness in carrying out the task that we have been assigned to do. 1 Peter 2:9 "But ye are a chosen generation, a royal priesthood, a holy nation, a peculiar people; that ye should shew forth the praises of him who hath called you out of darkness into his marvellous light:"

Continuous and constant fresh baptism of the Holy Spirit and Fire through our Lord Jesus Christ is the key to doing greater works than what our Lord Jesus did. The boldness comes only from Him to us through His Spirit.

The disciples of Jesus needed the Fire, and so do we now, more than ever, when sin and iniquities are escalating because the end is very close. In this latter time, if we are to be effective as God wants us to be, constant and fresh infilling of the Holy Spirit and fire is very important in order to run the race and fight the good fight. With the baptism of the Holy Spirit and Fire is the anointing of the Holy Spirit. When we have the Spirit of God in and on us, there are great tasks and assignments that God expects us to do. The anointing of the Holy Spirit is not to keep or to boast or show off; it is to reveal the mightiness and awesomeness of God and to demonstrate His power. The source of power, boldness, and ability to be an achiever for God, and to do the greater works that Jesus Christ desires us to do is to depend on the power of the Holy Spirit.

Therefore, let us continually seek the fresh infilling of the Holy Spirit and Fire so we may be vessels through which God's transformative power and love can flow to impact our world.

"The Spirit of the Lord GOD is upon me; because the LORD hath anointed me to preach good tidings unto the meek; he hath sent me to bind up the broken-hearted, to proclaim liberty to the captives, and the opening of the prison to them that are bound; To proclaim the acceptable year of the LORD, and the day of vengeance of our God; to comfort all that mourn; To appoint unto them that mourn in Zion, to give unto them beauty for ashes, the oil of joy for mourning, the garment of praise for the spirit of heaviness; that they might be called trees of righteousness, the planting of the LORD, that he might be glorified," according to Isaiah 61:1–3. John 14:12–14 also says, "Verily, verily, I say unto you, He that believeth on me, the works that I do shall he do also; and greater works than these shall he do; because I go unto my Father. And whatsoever ye shall ask in my name, that will I do, that the Father may be glorified in the Son. If ye shall ask any thing in my name, I will do it."

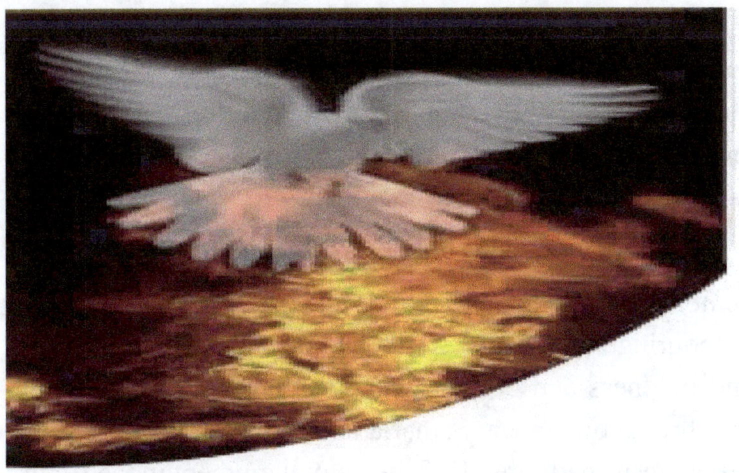

Acts 1:4-5, 8 states, "And, being assembled together with them, commanded them that they should not depart from Jerusalem, but wait for the promise of the Father, which, saith he, ye have heard of me. For John truly baptised with water; but ye shall be baptised with the Holy Ghost not many days hence. But ye shall receive power, after that the Holy Ghost has come upon you: and ye shall be witnesses unto me both in Jerusalem, and in all Judaea, and in Samaria, and unto the uttermost part of the earth." When the day of Pentecost fully came in Acts 2:1-4, it marked the beginning of what was said by Prophet Joel in his book.

Joel 2:28-32 declares, "And it shall come to pass afterward, that I will pour out my spirit upon all flesh; and your sons and your daughters shall prophesy, your old men shall dream dreams, your young men shall see visions: And also upon the servants and upon the handmaids in those days will I pour out my spirit. And I will shew wonders in the heavens and in the earth, blood, and fire, and pillars of smoke. The sun shall be turned into darkness, and the moon into blood, before the great and the terrible day of the LORD come. And it shall come to pass, that whosoever shall call on the name of the LORD shall be delivered: for in mount Zion and in Jerusalem shall be deliverance, as the LORD hath said, and in the remnant whom the LORD shall call."

Acts 2 and the fulfillment of Joel's prophecy demonstrate the inauguration of this new age, marked by the outpouring of the Holy Spirit. The disciples received power and boldness and became witnesses not only in Jerusalem but throughout Judea, Samaria and to the ends of the earth, just as Jesus had foretold. This pivotal moment in the Bible's narrative showcases the transformative and empowering work of the Holy Spirit in the lives of believers and the unfolding of God's divine plan.

Taking a look into Prophet Isaiah's vision, when he got the revelation of Heaven, and for him to be effective in God's business, he needed fire purification. Also was Prophet Ezekiel's call and Prophet Daniel's dream of the four beasts, all in Isaiah 6:1-9, Ezekiel 1, Ezekiel 2:1-3 and in Daniel 7:9-16.

Fire purification assures us of complete forgiveness of whatever sins we might have committed. It is the consecrating, setting apart and guaranteeing of a person being specially chosen and elected for a major responsibility. It is to prepare us for that important task of our existence and ensure that we are adequately prepared for the prompt and accurate declaration of the true Words of God with boldness and courage. The concept of fire purification, as seen in Isaiah's vision, serves as a powerful metaphor in the spiritual realm. It symbolises the process of cleansing and consecrating individuals for God's service. The purification of one's heart, mind and speech is essential to effectively convey God's message with boldness and sincerity. This purifying work ensures that those chosen for significant responsibilities are adequately prepared to carry out their tasks in accordance with God's will.

Indeed, the Lord equips and strengthens His messengers to confidently declare His message, free from fear and doubt, as they are empowered by His presence and His words. Amen.

CHAPTER FOUR - CONSUMING FIRE

Consume simply means used or destroyed up, total ravaging, devouring, complete absorption, engrossing or monopolising.[5] Our God, as the "Consuming Fire," consumes completely and does not and will not share us. The concept of God as the "Consuming Fire" carries profound implications for those who seek to understand His nature and the relationship between the divine and humanity. When we contemplate God's identity as a consuming fire, it highlights the absolute nature of His presence. This notion leaves no room for lukewarm devotion or partial commitment. He says, "For I the Lord thy God am a Jealous God" in Exodus 20:5. There is no chance for halfway consumption when God is involved; it is either you are consumed up or not at all. So, we find a clear declaration of His uncompromising nature. God's jealousy is not driven by insecurity but rather by His

---

[5] Consume, Merriam Webster, <https://www.merriam-webster.com/dictionary/consume>

desire for wholehearted devotion and obedience. Thus, when we approach God, we do so with the awareness that it is an all-encompassing journey. It is an acknowledgment that in His presence, there is no room for a divided heart; it is an all-or-nothing proposition.

Deuteronomy 4:24 says, "For the LORD thy God is a consuming fire, even a jealous God," while Hebrews 12:29 confirms it, saying, "For our God is a consuming fire." God is compared to fire, not only because of His glorious brightness but also on account of His anger against sin, which consumes sinners as fire does stubble, as written in Deuteronomy 32:21-22, saying, "They have moved me to jealousy with that which is not God; they have provoked me to anger with their vanities: and I will move them to jealousy with those which are not a people; I will provoke them to anger with a foolish nation. For a fire is kindled in mine anger, and shall burn unto the lowest hell, and shall consume the earth with her increase, and set on fire the foundations of the mountains," while Ezekiel 21:31-32 says, "And I will pour out mine indignation upon thee, I will blow against thee in the fire of my wrath, and deliver thee into the hand of brutish men, and skilful to destroy. Thou shalt be for fuel to the fire; thy blood shall be in the midst of the land; thou shalt be no more remembered: for I the LORD have spoken it."

This portrayal of God as a consuming fire, as reiterated in Deuteronomy 4:24 and Hebrews 12:29, extends beyond mere symbolism. It serves as a reminder that God's holiness and righteousness are like a refining fire that purges and consumes sin. This divine fire doesn't merely bring light and warmth, but, as described in Deuteronomy 32:21-22, it burns against ungodliness and consumes the works of darkness. In Ezekiel 21:31-32, we see the imagery of God's indignation as a fire that destroys and purifies, leaving no trace of impurity. This concept encourages believers to approach their faith with deep reverence and an understanding that God's consuming nature is not to be feared but embraced, for it refines, purifies and ultimately sets the heart ablaze with His love and righteousness. In this, we find the profound beauty of God's all-consuming presence, transforming lives and refining souls with an intensity that leaves no room for compromise.

In Isaiah 30:27-33 it says, "Behold, the name of the LORD cometh from far, burning with his anger, and the burden thereof is heavy: his lips are full of indignation, and his tongue as a devouring fire: And his breath, as an overflowing stream, shall reach to the midst of the neck, to sift the nations with the sieve of vanity: and there shall be a bridle in the jaws of the people, causing them to err. Ye shall have a song, as in the night when a holy solemnity is kept; and gladness of heart, as when one goeth with a pipe to come into the mountain of the LORD, to the mighty One of Israel. And the LORD shall cause his glorious voice to be heard, and shall shew the lighting down of his arm, with the indignation of his anger, and with the flame of a devouring fire, with scattering, and tempest, and hailstones. For through the voice of the LORD shall the Assyrian be beaten down, which smote with a rod. And in every place where the grounded staff shall pass, which the LORD shall lay upon him, it shall be with tabrets and harps: and in battles of shaking will he fight with it. For Tophet is ordained of old; yea, for the king it is prepared; he hath made it deep and large: the pile thereof is fire and much wood; the breath of the LORD, like a stream of brimstone, doth kindle it."

But when His glory comes down upon someone, or when He is revealing Himself in the demonstration of His power, or in Judgement like in the case of Sodom and Gomorrah, it is always an extraordinary, phenomenal, and outstanding occasion. Take, for instance, the visitation of God to His people at Mount Sinai and the demonstration of His power on Mount Carmel in order to make His people have genuine repentance. As well as the face of Stephen, the great man of faith, shining with the glory of God when he was seized for trial shortly before he died, to mention a few, according to the writings in Exodus 19:18-21: "And mount Sinai was altogether on a smoke, because the LORD descended upon it in fire: and the smoke thereof ascended as the smoke of a furnace, and the whole mount quaked greatly. And when the voice of the trumpet sounded long, and waxed louder and louder, Moses spake, and God answered him by a voice. And the LORD came down upon mount Sinai, on the top of the mount: and the LORD called Moses up to the top of the mount, and Moses went up. And the LORD said unto Moses, Go down, charge the people, lest they break through unto the LORD to gaze, and many of them perish."

Exodus 24:17 says, "And the sight of the glory of the LORD was like devouring fire on the top of the mount in the eyes of the children of Israel." Here, the image of this devouring fire serves as a powerful metaphor for the consuming and grand nature of God's glory. It signifies that when one stands in the presence of the Almighty, there is an overwhelming sense of God's holiness and power that cannot be casually approached. It is a reminder that God's glory is not something to be taken lightly but rather revered and approached with reverence and humility. And Exodus 34:29-33 states, "And it came to pass, when Moses came down from mount Sinai with the two tables of testimony in Moses' hand, when he came down from the mount, that Moses wist not that the skin of his face shone while he talked with him. And when Aaron and all the children of Israel saw Moses, behold, the skin of his face shone; and they were afraid to come nigh him. And Moses called unto them; and Aaron and all the rulers of the congregation returned unto him: and Moses talked with them. And afterward, all the children of Israel came nigh: and he gave them in commandment all that the LORD had spoken with him in mount Sinai. And till Moses had done speaking with them, he put a veil on his face." The scripture suggests that there are layers to God's revelation, and the veil represents a barrier between the finite understanding of humanity and the infinite nature of God. This narrative deepens our understanding of the consuming fire of God's glory, emphasising that while it transforms and radiates, it also respects the limitations of human capacity in comprehending the divine.

In 1 Kings 18:30-39, it says, And Elijah said unto all the people, Come near unto me. And all the people came near unto him. And he repaired the altar of the LORD that was broken down. And Elijah took twelve stones, according to the number of the tribes of the sons of Jacob, unto whom the word of the LORD came, saying, Israel shall be thy name: And with the stones he built an altar in the name of the LORD: and he made a trench about the altar, as great as would contain two measures of seed. And he put the wood in order, and cut the bullock in pieces, and laid him on the wood, and said, Fill four barrels with water, and pour it on the burnt sacrifice, and on the wood. And he said, Do it the second time. And they did it the second time. And he said, Do it the third time. And they did it the third time. And the water ran round about the altar, and he filled the trench also with water. And it came to pass at the time of the offering of the evening sacrifice, that Elijah the prophet came near, and said, LORD God of Abraham, Isaac, and of Israel, let it be known this day that thou art God in Israel, and that I am thy servant, and that I have done all these things at thy word. Hear me, O LORD, hear me, that this people may know that thou art the LORD God, and that thou hast turned their heart back again. Then the fire of the LORD fell, and consumed the burnt sacrifice, and the wood, and the stones, and the dust, and licked up the water that was in the trench. And when all the people saw it, they fell on their faces: and they said, The LORD, he is the God; the LORD, he is the God."

And Acts 6: 8, 10 and 15 declare, "And Stephen, full of faith and power, did great wonders and miracles among the people. And they were not able to resist the wisdom and the spirit by which he spake. And all that sat in the council, looking stedfastly on him, saw his face as it had been the face of an angel." This is phenomenal!

Just as in the previous passages, we see the concept of an individual being consumed or transformed by a divine presence, reminding us that individuals who walk closely with God can bear witness to His glory and be conduits of His power and wisdom, leaving an ineffaceable impact on those around them.

In the Old Testament, the presence of fire and or the consumption of offerings by flame confirms God's presence and that He is involved and accepts the people's sacrifices or offerings. Judges 6:21-24 says, "Then the angel of the LORD put forth the end of the staff that was in his hand and touched the flesh and the unleavened cakes, and there rose up fire out of the rock and consumed the flesh and the unleavened cakes. Then the angel of the LORD departed out of his sight. And when Gideon perceived that he was an angel of the LORD, Gideon said, Alas, O Lord GOD! For because I have seen an angel of the LORD face to face. And the LORD said unto him, Peace be unto thee; fear not: thou shalt not die. Then Gideon built an altar there unto the LORD, and called it Jehovah-shalom: unto this day it is yet in Ophrah of the Abi-ezrites." There are numerous references to fire in the Bible, which emphasise God's purification and Judgement on wickedness and unbelief.

Our God, as the "consuming fire," cannot behold iniquities, hates and judges evil with the wicked acts of man.

But He is full of great love and marvellous compassion for mankind, His handwork. He desires that we be saved from all the atrocities of the devil, from the ungodly and wicked men, from perishing, damnation to hell, and from eternal death. The prophet Amos warned Israel to live righteously for God. He said in Amos 5:6, "Seek the Lord and ye shall live; lest He break out like a fire in the house of Joseph and devour it, and there be none to quench it in Bethel." If we are integrous and we allow ourselves to be completely consumed by God for His own purpose and glory, then we will be a mighty and powerful instrument in His hands, bringing honour, praise, and glory to Him. Let us allow the zeal of God to consume us, to burn in our souls with a burning force that cannot be quenched or hindered, and as a fire that cannot be quenched or stopped. Oh Hallelujah!

CHAPTER FIVE – GOD'S SERVANTS AS FLAMES OF FIRE

A flame of fire is the chosen symbol of the holiness of God, as indicated by Exodus 3:2 and Revelation 2:18, making known the intense, all-consuming operation of his holiness in relation to sin. A flame is a visible light, a glowing hot matter. It is self-sustaining and produces energy. The glow of a flame is complex, and the colour depends on temperature and the dominant colour in a flame changes with temperature. This variance in colours within a flame is not only fascinating but also holds practical significance in fields such as chemistry, where the different colours of flames are used to identify elements and compounds.

Fire and flame are closely associated with Israel's worship and religious life. According to God's instruction, a fire was kept burning continuously on the altars where burnt offerings were sacrificed. The consumption of offerings by flame indicates God's involvement and acceptance of their sacrifices for this and many other reasons; we need to know and understand the importance and the essentiality of God making His servants Flames of fire. Servants of God who have been set apart or instituted into a sacred office and have come to the realisation of their purpose and God's plan for themselves in life need to walk in the realisation of who they are and what they are supposed to do or be like when He made them to be Flames of Fire. We should always realise that the angels of God always encamp round about us when allowed, attending, assisting, ministering, and in constant war-fare over us and that at our command through Jesus Christ, they yield to our bidding in ministering to us. So God, in making His angels winds, provides a sure, constant, and guaranteed assistance for the Flames of Fire to be on always paraphrasing Hebrews 1:7, which says, "In speaking of the angels he says, "He makes his angels winds, his servants flames of fire" and in Psalm 104:4 it is written "He makes winds his messengers (or angels), flames of fire his servants." (NIV)

Hence, these scriptural passages compare angels to winds and flames of fire to God's servant, highlighting the idea that God's celestial messengers are always ready to assist and empower those who are dedicated to serving Him faithfully.

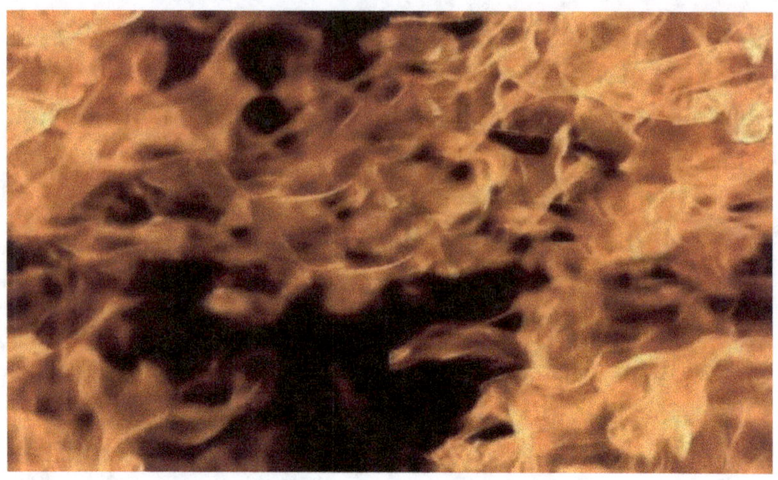

Servants of God as flames of fire carry an undeniable special and dangerous anointing, and they are not to be joked with irrespective of who they are, regarding race, sex, age or colour or their position in whatever lineage they occupy, take, for example, the opposition of Miriam and Aaron against Moses where she was afflicted with leprosy and confinement in Numbers 12: 6-12. "And he said, Hear now my words: If there be a prophet among you, I the LORD will make myself known unto him in a vision, and will speak unto him in a dream. My servant Moses is not so, who is faithful in all mine house. With him will I speak mouth to mouth, even apparently, and not in dark speeches; and the similitude of the LORD shall he behold: wherefore then were ye not afraid to speak against my servant Moses? And the anger of the LORD was kindled against them, and he departed. And the cloud departed from off the tabernacle; and, behold, Miriam became leprous, white as snow: and Aaron looked upon Miriam, and, behold, she was leprous. And Aaron said unto Moses, Alas, my lord, I beseech thee, lay not the sin upon us, wherein we have done foolishly, and wherein we have sinned." This incident emphasises the need to respect the responsibilities of God's selected servants. There is no turning back when God chooses someone, irrespective of what human feelings might be. His word is yea and Amen, for the calling of God is without repentance, and due to this, many have brought a lot of setbacks, disasters, afflictions, barrenness, stagnation of various forms, and lack of progress of various degrees to themselves; probably or inclusive to their families and their communities both physically and spiritually beyond their comprehension because they have kicked against the thorns and the apple of God's eyes.

Or is it the rebellion and the murmuring of Korah, Dathan and Abiram against the leadership of Moses when the earth swallowed them up in Numbers 16:29-35 saying, "If these men die the common death of all men, or if they be visited after the visitation of all men; then the LORD hath not sent me. But if the LORD make a new thing and the earth open her mouth, and swallow them up, with all that appertain unto them, and they go down quick into the pit; then ye shall understand that these men have provoked the LORD. And it came to pass, as he had made an end of speaking all these words, that the ground clave asunder that was under them: And the earth opened her mouth and swallowed them up, and their houses, and all the men that appertained unto Korah, and all their goods. They, and all that appertained to them, went down alive into the pit, and the earth closed upon them, and they perished from among the congregation. And all Israel that were round about them fled at the cry of them: for they said, Lest the earth swallow us up also. And there came out a fire from the LORD, and consumed the two hundred and fifty men that offered incense". It is a fearful thing to fall into the hands of the living God. Hebrews 10:31.

Therefore, when individuals resist the calling of God and persist in going against His divine plan, they may unknowingly set in motion a chain of events that could lead to unintended consequences. Their defiance against God's purpose often results in a disconnection from the divine guidance and blessings that were meant to accompany them on their life's journey. As they continue to walk in opposition to God's will, they may find themselves trapped in cycles of hardship, despair, and frustration. However, it's essential to remember that God's grace and mercy are always available for those who humbly seek His guidance and turn back to His intended path. Through repentance and a willingness to follow His calling, individuals can find restoration, renewed purpose, and the abundant life that God had originally planned for them.

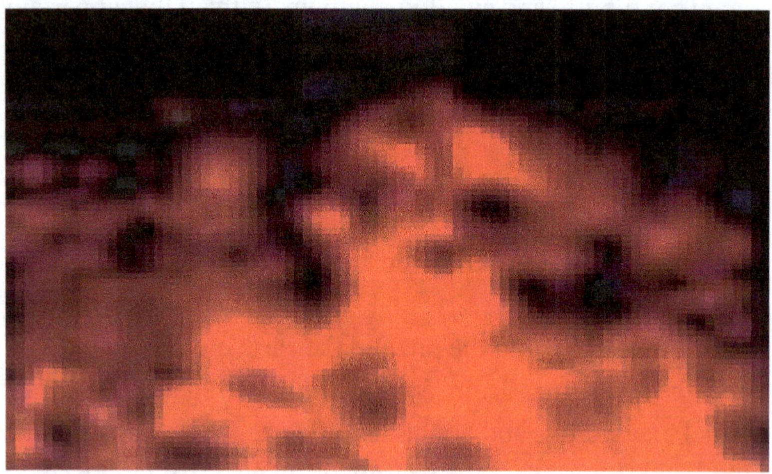

What about the lies of Ananias and Sapphira in Acts 5:1- 12: "But a certain man named Ananias, with Sapphira, his wife, sold a possession, And kept back part of the price, his wife also being privy to it, and brought a certain part, and laid it at the apostles' feet. But Peter said, Ananias, why hath Satan filled thine heart to lie to the Holy Ghost and to keep back part of the price of the land? While it remained, was it not thine own? And after it was sold, was it not in thine own power? Why hast thou conceived this thing in thine heart? Thou hast not lied unto men but unto God.

And Ananias, hearing these words, fell down, and gave up the ghost: and great fear came on all them that heard these things. And the young men arose, wound him up, and carried him out, and buried him. And it was about the space of three hours after when his wife, not knowing what was done, came in. And Peter answered unto her, Tell me whether ye sold the land for so much? And she said, Yea, for so much. Then Peter said unto her, How is it that ye have agreed together to tempt the Spirit of the Lord? Behold, the feet of them which have buried thy husband are at the door and shall carry thee out. Then fell she down straightway at his feet, and yielded up the ghost: and the young men came in and found her dead, and, carrying her forth, buried her by her husband. And great fear came upon all the church, and upon as many as heard these things. And by the hands of the apostles were many signs and wonders wrought among the people; (and they were all with one accord in Solomon's porch."

This story serves as a cautionary tale in early Christian history, underscoring the importance of honesty and integrity in one's dealings within the faith community and with God. It also underscores the significance of respecting the presence of the Holy Spirit within the Christian community.

In the Bible, the Lord said in 1 Chronicles 16:22, "Saying, Touch not mine anointed, and do my prophets no harm," and confirms it again in Psalm 105:15, "Saying, Touch not mine anointed, and do my prophets no harm." Meanwhile, through proper respect and humble handling of the anointed ones, the anointing should be a yoke lifter and destroyer, hereby bringing various kinds of deliverance. Isaiah 10:27 says, "And it shall come to pass in that day, that his burden shall be taken away from off thy shoulder, and his yoke from off thy neck, and the yoke shall be destroyed because of the anointing." When someone comes in contact with a 'genuine' servant of God, there must be a remarkable change. God, in dwelling within His temple, that is, within His people, makes them as active and powerful as the "flames" of fire that is generated from Himself, who is the greater one who lives on the inside. Fire thus serves various purposes. Flames of fire in its functions, when around a right, proper and yielding field or medium, in describing a prepared heart, sets him or her on fire by the process of anointing transference.

Symbolically, fire is an emblem or indication of the divine process of responsibility effected upon the spiritual natures of persons in covenant with God. This person is set on fire and continues to burn for God and all useless, unwanted weeds, self and every form of carnalities, articles and elements that hinder the proper glorious growth of worthiness, edification, fruitfulness, multiplications, excellencies, dignity and valuable substances in the life of a yielding, spiritual person are gradually pruned off. It's a reminder that through trials and challenges, a person's faith and devotion can become even more resolute and pure, ultimately leading to a life characterized by spiritual growth, virtue, and a closer relationship with God. This transformation is often seen as a necessary and ongoing part of the spiritual journey for those in covenant with God.

John 15:1-3 says, "I am the true vine, and my Father is the gardener. He cuts off every branch in me that bears no fruit, while every branch that does bear fruit he prunes so that it will be even more fruitful. You are already clean because of the word I have spoken to you." (NIV). It then consumes, and the process continues.

This fire is to be understood as the instrument of divine judgement, which judges and destroys every wicked act of disobedience in lives. The contact with these flames leaves people free by destroying all those buying and selling demons that attach to a Christian. When in contact with resisting wicked evil spirits, it is either they are destroyed, or they disappear to a far place, fleeing that arena due to the hot and charged spiritual atmosphere that creates an uncomfortable environment for their manifestation. Ministering as Flames of Fire is serving under the powerful anointing of the Holy Spirit. When a servant of God in any situation releases the Word of God, the condition must change, and there must be remarkable signs and wonders following no matter how difficult it looks because the Lord said in Jeremiah 23:29, "Is not my word like as a fire? saith the LORD; and like a hammer that breaketh the rock in pieces?" Nothing is impossible for God to do, and through ministry as Flames of Fire, believers can witness the miraculous and transformative work of the Holy Spirit in the lives of those they serve.

CHAPTER SIX – BENEFITS OF GOD'S FIRE ON A CHOSEN ONE

The fire of God's presence on a chosen one means having the anointing of God. What now are the benefits of God's anointing on us? The Scripture says by the anointing, Jesus breaks the yoke, and by the Holy Ghost and His power just as the prophets had said, and this now is the day, the hour, the time, and the season of the latter rain. God said, "And I will shake all nations, and the desire of all nations shall come: and I will fill this house with glory, saith the LORD of hosts. The silver is mine, and the gold is mine, saith the LORD of hosts. The glory of this latter house shall be greater than of the former, saith the LORD of hosts: and in this place will I give peace, saith the LORD of hosts. Is the seed yet in the barn? Yea, as yet the vine, and the fig tree, and the pomegranate, and the olive tree, hath not brought forth: from this day will I bless you. Speak to Zerubbabel, governor of Judah, saying, I will shake the heavens and the earth; And I will overthrow the throne of kingdoms, and I will destroy the strength of the kingdoms of the heathen; and I will overthrow the chariots, and those that ride in them; and the horses and their riders shall come down, everyone by the sword of his brother. In that day, saith the LORD of hosts, will I take thee, O Zerubbabel, my servant, the son of Shealtiel, saith the LORD, and will make thee as a signet: for I have chosen thee, saith the LORD of hosts," as written in Haggai 2: 7-9; 19-23.

These verses from the book of Haggai remind us of the profound and timeless truth that God's promises and blessings are certain. In times of adversity and challenges, when it seems like the fruits of our labour are yet to come, we can find solace in the knowledge that the Lord is at work in the background, preparing to bestow His abundant blessings upon us. Zerubbabel's journey from servant to signet is a testament to God's transformative power and His commitment to those who serve Him with devotion. Just as Zerubbabel's story reflects God's divine plan, it encourages us to remain steadfast in our faith, knowing that in due time, the heavens and the earth will be shaken in our favor, and we too will be elevated to become a signet of His grace in the world.

The Lord is pouring out His Spirit on all flesh, and great things are happening. The Lord has released in and on us His divine authority, power, and glory, sanctifying us by the Truth of His Word, giving us dominion over kingdoms and thrones, abundant blessings and great supplies, protection and deliverance, favours and breakthroughs.

Quoting Matthew 28:18, it is written, "Then Jesus came to them and said, "All authority in heaven and on earth has been given to me" and in sure confidence of the tasks given and full support from Him, Jesus in His own words said with emphasis: "And these signs will accompany those who believe: In my name, they will drive out demons; they will speak in new tongues; they will pick up snakes with their hands; and when they drink deadly poison, it will not hurt them at all; they will place their hands on sick people, and they will getwell," and in Mark 16:17- 18 (NIV).

The above verses from Matthew and Mark remind us of the immense authority and power vested in Jesus Christ, the source of our faith. They explain the extraordinary signs and wonders that can manifest through unwavering belief and trust in Him. These verses inspire us to walk in faith and embrace our calling with confidence, knowing that with His support, we can face any challenge, even those that seem insurmountable. Just as Zerubbabel was chosen as a signet by the Lord to carry out His divine plan, believers, too, are empowered by Jesus to carry out miraculous acts and serve as beacons of His grace, ultimately fulfilling His greater purpose in the world.

In John 17: 9- 11 (NIV), Jesus said, "I pray for them. I am not praying for the world but for those you have given me, for they are yours. All I have is yours, and all you have is mine. And glory has come to me through them. I will remain in the world no longer, but they are still in the world, and I am coming to you. Holy Father, protect them by the power of your name, the name you gave me, so that they may be one as we are one."

And as stated in John 17: 17-25 (NIV), "Sanctify them by the truth; your word is truth. As you sent me into the world, I have sent them into the world. For them, I sanctify myself, that they too may be truly sanctified. I have given them the glory that you gave me, that they may be one as we are one: I in them and you in me. May they be brought to complete unity to let the world know that you sent me and have loved them even as you have loved me.

Father, I want those you have given me to be with me where I am and to see my glory, the glory you have given me because you loved me before the creation of the world. Righteous Father, though the world does not know you, I know you, and they know that you have sent me."

It has been predestined before the creation of this world, as poignantly revealed in Romans 8:28-31, saying, "And we know that all things work together for good to them that love God, to them who are the called according to his purpose. For whom he did foreknow, he also did predestinate to be conformed to the image of his Son, that he might be the firstborn among many brethren. Moreover, whom he did predestinate, them he also called: and whom he called, them he also justified: and whom he justified, them he also glorified. What shall we then say to these things? If God be for us, who can be against us?"

Jeremiah, in his words, said, "Then the word of the LORD came unto me, saying, before I formed thee in the belly I knew thee, and before thou camest forth out of the womb I sanctified thee, and I ordained thee a prophet unto the nations. Then the LORD put forth his hand and touched my mouth. And the LORD said unto me, Behold, I have put my words in thy mouth. See, I have this day set thee over the nations and over the kingdoms, to root out, and to pull down, and to destroy, and to throw down, to build, and to plant. Moreover, the word of the LORD came unto me, saying, Jeremiah, what seest thou? And I said, I see a rod of an almond tree. Then said the LORD unto me, Thou hast well seen: for I will hasten my word to perform it. For, behold, I have made thee this day a defenced city, and an iron pillar, and brazen walls against the whole land, against the kings of Judah, against the princes thereof, against the priests thereof, and against the people of the land. And they shall fight against thee, but they shall not prevail against thee; for I am with thee, saith the LORD, to deliver thee." (Jeremiah1:4-5; 9-12; 18-19)

While Isaiah prophesied saying, "Thus saith the LORD to his anointed, to Cyrus, whose right hand I have holden, to subdue nations before him; and I will loose the loins of kings, to open before him the two leaved gates; and the gates shall not be shut; I will go before thee, and make the crooked places straight: I will break in pieces the gates of brass, and cut in sunder the bars of iron: And I will give thee the treasures of darkness, and hidden riches of secret places, that thou mayest know that I, the LORD, which call thee by thy name, am the God of Israel. For Jacob my servant's sake, and Israel mine elect, I have even called thee by thy name: I have surnamed thee, though thou hast not known me. I am the LORD, and there is none else, there is no God beside me: I girded thee, though thou hast not known me: That they may know from the rising of the sun, and from the west, that there is none beside me. I am the LORD, and there is none else" (Isaiah 45:1- 6).

Guidance- God spoke to Moses in the burning bush experience and called him to lead the children of Israel out of Egyptian bondage in Exodus 3:2-12. Afterwards, He also used fire to guide His people. The Bible made us know that in the wanderings of the Israelites in the wilderness, they relied each night on a PILLAR OF FIRE from heaven to guide them in their travels. As believers in this world, we are on assignment to represent our home and land. The Bible made us know that we do not belong here, and so on this journey of ours, we have to depend on that fire source for many activities. God's protection is an additional guarantee for His people. God declares in Zechariah 2:5; 8-9, saying, "For I, saith the LORD, will be unto her a wall of fire round about, and will be the glory in the midst of her. For thus saith the LORD of hosts; After the glory hath he sent me unto the nations which spoiled you: for he that toucheth you toucheth the apple of his eye. For, behold, I will shake mine hand upon them, and they shall be a spoil to their servants: and ye shall know that the LORD of hosts hath sent me."

Victorious and overcoming: In reference to Obadiah 1:17-18, fire is illustrative of the church overcoming her enemies using and depending on the Word of God to get their victories. He categorically declared that upon Mount Zion shall be deliverance, and there shall be holiness; and the house of Jacob shall possess their possessions. And the house of Jacob shall be a fire, and the house of Joseph a flame, and the house of Esau for stubble, and they shall kindle in them, and devour them; and there shall not be any remaining of the house of Esau; for the LORD hath spoken it while Jeremiah 5:14 says, "Wherefore thus saith the LORD God of hosts, because ye speak this word, behold, I will make my words in thy mouth fire, and this people wood, and it shall devour them. Is not my word like as a fire? saith the LORD; and like a hammer that breaketh the rock in pieces?"

Therefore, the church, when grounded in the Word of God and led by His divine guidance, can conquer its adversaries and overcome challenges. The imagery of fire in these verses signifies the refining and purifying nature of God's Word, which not only consumes the forces of evil but also empowers believers to possess their spiritual inheritance. In a world where spiritual battles are ever-present, these verses serve as a reminder of the church's strength and the unwavering authority of God's Word, which can break through even the hardest of hearts and establish holiness and deliverance for those who trust in it.

Therefore, with all these emphasised words of God, it is obvious that it is an essentiality of life for us as servants (believers) to remain in the presence of God, keeping the fire burning in the Holy Ghost. A genuine fire-filled believer should not allow it to go down and give any chance to the devil by being spitted out by God. Revelation 3:15–22 says, "I know thy works, that thou art neither cold nor hot: I would thou wert cold or hot. So then, because thou art lukewarm and neither cold nor hot, I will spue thee out of my mouth. Because thou sayest, I am rich, and increased with goods, and have need of nothing; and knowest not that thou art wretched, and miserable, and poor, and blind, and naked: I counsel thee to buy of me gold tried in the fire, that thou mayest be rich; and white raiment, that thou mayest be clothed, and that the shame of thy nakedness do not appear; and anoint thine eyes with eyesalve, that thou mayest see. As many as I love, I rebuke and chasten: be zealous, therefore, and repent. Behold, I stand at the door and knock: if any man hear my voice and open the door, I will come into him and will sup with him, and he with me. To him that overcometh will I grant to sit with me in my throne, even as I also overcame, and am set down with my Father in his throne. He that hath an ear, let him hear what the Spirit saith unto the churches." Leviticus 6:13 instructed us that the fire shall ever be burning upon the altar; it shall never go out. So, to be hot constantly for the Lord, we need to remain fixed and completely connected, drawing continuously close to Him, deriving the strength and ability that is necessary for day-to-day activities. 'Then is the victory guaranteed.'

Destroys Rebellion.

Fire from heaven is described as an instrument of God's wrath to fight for His people and to crush the satanic rebellion. Revelation 20: 9-10 says, "And they went up on the breadth of the earth and compassed the camp of the saints about, and the beloved city: and fire came down from God out of heaven, and devoured them. And the devil that deceived them was cast into the lake of fire and brimstone, where the beast and the false prophet are, and shall be tormented day and night forever and ever. Amen."

These verses from Revelation vividly portray the final battle between good and evil, where the divine fire from heaven represents God's ultimate authority and judgment. The symbolism of fire as an instrument of divine wrath serves as a powerful reminder that God's justice prevails and evil will ultimately be defeated. It underscores the importance of faith and righteousness in a world where spiritual warfare is a constant reality. As believers, we should find solace in the assurance that just as God's fire will consume the forces of darkness, His love and protection will continue to shield the faithful, ultimately leading to the triumph of good over evil and the eternal peace of the beloved city.

CHAPTER SEVEN - REALITY OF HELLFIRE

Hell is the place where wicked people go when they die. It is the place created for the eternal imprisonment of wickedness, suffering, or punishment. The place of eternal punishment for the unrighteous. Hell is "a lake of fire burning with brimstone." Brimstone is a type of sulphur, a yellowish mineral and is highly combustible.[6]

This description of hell symbolises the intensity of suffering that awaits those who deviate from moral righteousness. Despite the diverse interpretations of hell, the overarching theme revolves around the consequences of a life marked by sin and malevolence, thus serving as a stark reminder of the importance of moral conduct and the potential ramifications of straying from the path of virtue.

---

[6] Fire and brimstone,
<https://en.wikipedia.org/wiki/Fire_and_brimstone>

The NKJV and KJV use this word to translate Sheol and Hades, the Old and New Testament words, respectively, for the abode of the dead. In the New Testament, eternal damnation is pictured as an everlasting fire. Hell as a place of punishment translates Gehenna, the Greek form of the Hebrew word that means "the vale of Hinnom" – a valley just south of Jerusalem. In this valley, the Canaanites worshipped Baal and the fire-god Molech by sacrificing their children in a fire that burned continuously. Even Ahaz and Manasseh, kings of Judah, were guilty of this terrible, idolatrous practice, as written in 2 Chronicles 28:3 and 2 Chronicles 33:6, saying, "Moreover he burnt incense in the valley of the son of Hinnom, and burnt his children in the fire, after the abominations of the heathen whom the LORD had cast out before the children of Israel. And he caused his children to pass through the fire in the valley of the son of Hinnom: also he observed times, and used enchantments, and used witchcraft, and dealt with a familiar spirit, and with wizards: he wrought much evil in the sight of the LORD, to provoke him to anger."

Hence, these actions, collectively described as wrought much evil in the sight of the LORD, underscore the severity of the kings' departure from their spiritual obligations. The narrative essentially emphasises the consequences that befall those who abandon the moral teachings of their faith and indulge in practices deemed abominable by the divine.

The prophet Jeremiah predicted that God would visit such destruction upon Jerusalem that this valley would be known as the "Valley of Slaughter," according to Jeremiah 7:31-34, "And they have built the high places of Tophet, which is in the valley of the son of Hinnom, to burn their sons and their daughters in the fire; which I commanded them not, neither came it into my heart. Therefore, behold, the days come, saith the LORD, that it shall no more be called Tophet, nor the valley of the son of Hinnom, but the valley of slaughter: for they shall bury in Tophet, till there be no place. And the carcases of this people shall be meat for the fowls of the heaven, and for the beasts of the earth; and none shall fray them away. Then will I cause to cease from the cities of Judah, and from the streets of Jerusalem, the voice of mirth, and the voice of gladness, the voice of the bridegroom, and the voice of the bride: for the land shall be desolate."

Similarly, Jeremiah 19:2-6 says, "And go forth unto the valley of the son of Hinnom, which is by the entry of the east gate, and proclaim there the words that I shall tell thee, And say, Hear ye the word of the LORD, O kings of Judah, and inhabitants of Jerusalem; Thus saith the LORD of hosts, the God of Israel; Behold, I will bring evil upon this place, the which whosoever heareth, his ears shall tingle. Because they have forsaken me, and have estranged this place, and have burned incense in it unto other gods, whom neither they nor their fathers have known, nor the kings of Judah, and have filled this place with the blood of innocents; They have also built the high places of Baal, to burn their sons with fire for burnt offerings unto Baal, which I commanded not, nor spake it, neither came it into my mind: Therefore, behold, the days come, saith the LORD, that this place shall no more be called Tophet, nor The valley of the son of Hinnom, but The valley of slaughter."

The core of the divine rebuke lies in the people's abandonment of the Lord, as they have forsaken Him, estranged the sacred grounds, and defiled it by burning incense to unknown gods. The sins committed in this valley include not only idolatry but also the shedding of innocent blood, a grievous offence that further deepens the divine displeasure. As a consequence of these evils, the valley of the son of Hinnom is prophesied to undergo a transformation. It will cease to be known as Tophet or the Valley of the Son of Hinnom; instead, it will be rebranded as the Valley of Slaughter.

So, in King Josiah's religious reforms, he put an end to this worship. He defiled the valley in order to make it unfit even for pagan worship. II Kings 23:10 declared, "And he defiled Topheth, which is in the valley of the children of Hinnom, that no man might make his son or his daughter pass through the fire to Molech."

In the time of Jesus, the Valley of Hinnom was used as the garbage dump of Jerusalem. Into it were thrown all the filth and garbage of the city, including the dead bodies of animals and executed criminals. To consume all this, fires burned constantly. Maggots worked in the filth. When the wind blew from that direction over the city, its awfulness was quite evident. At night, wild dogs howled and gnashed their teeth as they fought over the garbage. Jesus used this awful scene as a symbol of hell. In effect, he said, "Do you want to know what the hell is like? Look at the valley of Gehenna." So, hell may be described as God's "cosmic garbage dump." In this conceptualization, hell becomes the ultimate destination for all that is deemed unworthy of heaven, a repository for spiritual refuse. The recurrence of the term Gehenna in the New Testament, approximately 12 times, is enough to comprehend the significance of this metaphor in Jesus' teachings.

Each time, it is translated as "hell." With the exception of James 3:6: "And the tongue is a fire, a world of iniquity: so is the tongue among our members, that it defileth the whole body, and setteth on fire the course of nature; and it is set on fire of hell."

Only Jesus in the Bible used the word hell. Matthew 5:20-30 says, "But I say unto you, That whosoever is angry with his brother without a cause shall be in danger of the judgement: and whosoever shall say to his brother, Raca, shall be in danger of the council: but whosoever shall say, Thou fool, shall be in danger of hell fire. Therefore, if thou bring thy gift to the altar, and there rememberest that thy brother hath ought against thee; Leave there thy gift before the altar, and go thy way; first, be reconciled to thy brother, and then come and offer thy gift. Agree with thine adversary quickly, while thou art in the way with him; lest at any time the adversary deliver thee to the judge, and the judge deliver thee to the officer, and thou be cast into prison. Verily I say unto thee, Thou shalt by no means come out thence, till thou hast paid the uttermost farthing. Ye have heard that it was said by them of old time, Thou shalt not commit adultery: But I say unto you, That whosoever looketh on a woman to lust after her hath committed adultery with her already in his heart. And if thy right eye offend thee, pluck it out, and cast it from thee: for it is profitable for thee that one of thy members should perish, and not that thy whole body should be cast into hell. And if thy right hand offend thee, cut it off, and cast it from thee: for it is profitable for thee that one of thy members should perish, and not that thy whole body should be cast into hell."

Through these teachings, Jesus continuously establishes a connection between moral choices, internal disposition and the ultimate consequence of separation from God represented by hell. This profound engagement with the concept of hell in the moral and spiritual context demonstrates Jesus' peculiar emphasis on the importance of inner righteousness and the gravity of choices in determining one's eternal destiny.

It is written in Matthew 10:28: "And fear not them which kill the body, but are not able to kill the soul: but rather fear him which is able to destroy both soul and body in hell."

Also, Matthew 23:15-33 says: "Woe unto you, scribes and Pharisees, hypocrites! for ye compass sea and land to make one proselyte, and when he is made, ye make him twofold more the child of hell than yourselves. Woe unto you, ye blind guides, which say, Whosoever shall swear by the temple, it is nothing; but whosoever shall swear by the gold of the temple, he is a debtor! Ye fools and blind: for whether is greater, the gold, or the temple that sanctifieth the gold? And, Whosoever shall swear by the altar, it is nothing; but whosoever sweareth by the gift that is upon it, he is guilty. Ye fools and blind: for whether is greater, the gift, or the altar that sanctifieth the gift? Whoso therefore shall swear by the altar, sweareth by it, and by all things thereon. And whoso shall swear by the temple, sweareth by it, and by him that dwelleth therein. And he that shall swear by heaven, sweareth by the throne of God, and by him that sitteth thereon. Woe unto you, scribes and Pharisees, hypocrites! for ye pay tithe of mint and anise and cummin, and have omitted the weightier matters of the law, judgment, mercy, and faith: these ought ye to have done, and not to leave the other undone. Ye blind guides, which strain at a gnat and swallow a camel. Woe unto you, scribes and Pharisees, hypocrites! For ye make clean the outside of the cup and of the platter, but within, they are full of extortion and excess. Thou blind Pharisee, cleanse first that which is within the cup and platter, that the outside of them may be clean also. Woe unto you, scribes and Pharisees, hypocrites! for ye are like unto whited sepulchres, which indeed appear beautiful outward, but are within full of dead men's bones, and of all uncleanness. Even so, ye also outwardly appear righteous unto men, but within ye are full of hypocrisy and iniquity. Woe unto you, scribes and Pharisees, hypocrites! Because ye build the tombs of the prophets and garnish the sepulchres of the righteous, And say, if we had been in the days of our fathers, we would not have been partakers with them in the blood of the prophets. Wherefore ye be witnesses unto yourselves, that ye are the children of them which killed the prophets. Fill ye up then the measure of your fathers. Ye serpents, ye generation of vipers, how can ye escape the damnation of hell?"

Moreover, Mark 9:43-47 says: "And if thy hand offend thee, cut it off: it is better for thee to enter into life maimed than having two hands to go into hell, into the fire that never shall be quenched: Where their worm dieth not, and the fire is not quenched. And if thy foot offend thee, cut it off: it is better for thee to enter halt into life than having two feet to be cast into hell, into the fire that never shall be quenched: Where their worm dieth not, and the fire is not quenched. And if thine eye offend thee, pluck it out: it is better for thee to enter into the kingdom of God with one eye than having two eyes to be cast into hell fire."

The juxtaposition of the term "hell" with the modifier "fire" in certain scriptural passages, as in the reference to "hell fire," intensifies the concept. This coupling emphasises vivid and relentless imagery of punishment associated with the term "Gehenna." It's noteworthy that these descriptions of hell, portrayed in the New Testament, are attributed to the divine teachings of Jesus—depicting a striking paradox within the essence of infinite love.

Looking at the above passages, hell is also described as a place where "their worm does not die, and the fire is not quenched." This encapsulates a sense of perpetual torment, suggesting an unending state of anguish and suffering in the afterlife.

Repeatedly, Jesus spoke of outer darkness and a furnace of fire, where there will be wailing, weeping and gnashing of teeth. Matthew 22:13 informed us, "Then said the king to the servants, bind him hand and foot and take him away, and cast him into outer darkness; there shall be weeping and gnashing of teeth," and in Luke 12:5, it says, "But I will forewarn you whom ye shall fear: Fear him, which after he hath killed hath power to cast into hell; yea, I say unto you, Fear him" because according to Luke 13:28: "There shall be weeping and gnashing of teeth when ye shall see Abraham, and Isaac, and Jacob, and all the prophets, in the kingdom of God, and you yourselves thrust out."

These same scriptures are written in alliance with Matthew 18:9, which says, "And if your eye causes you to sin, pluck it out and cast *it* from you. It is better for you to enter into life with one eye, rather than having two eyes, to be cast into hell fire;" and Matthew 8:12 says: "But the sons of the kingdom will be cast out into outer darkness. There will be weeping and gnashing of teeth."

Furthermore, Matthew 13:42-50 says, "And will cast them into the furnace of fire. There will be wailing and gnashing of teeth. Then the righteous will shine forth as the sun in the kingdom of their Father. He who has ears to hear, let him hear! Again, the kingdom of heaven is like treasure hidden in a field, which a man found and hid, and for joy over it, he goes and sells all that he has and buys that field. Again, the kingdom of heaven is like a merchant seeking beautiful pearls, who, when he had found one pearl of great price, went and sold all that he had and bought it. Again, the kingdom of heaven is like a dragnet that was cast into the sea and gathered some of every kind, which, when it was full, they drew to shore, and they sat down and gathered the good into vessels but threw the bad away. So it will be at the end of the age. The angels will come forth, separate the wicked from among the just, and cast them into the furnace of fire. There will be wailing and gnashing of teeth."

Matthew 24:51 says, "He will cut him in two and appoint *him* his portion with the hypocrites. There shall be weeping and gnashing of teeth." And Matthew 25:30 states, "And cast the unprofitable servant into the outer darkness. There will be weeping and gnashing of teeth."

Obviously, this picture is drawn from the valley of Gehenna. The Book of Revelation describes hell as "a lake of fire burning with brimstone," according to Revelation 19:20, which states, "And the beast was taken, and with him the false prophet that wrought miracles before him, with which he deceived them that had received the mark of the beast, and them that worshipped his image. These both were cast alive into a lake of fire burning with brimstone," while Revelation 20:10-15 says, "And the devil that deceived them was cast into the lake of fire and brimstone, where the beast and the false prophet are, and shall be tormented day and night forever and ever. And I saw a great white throne, and him that sat on it, from whose face the earth and the heaven fled away; and there was found no place for them. And I saw the dead, small and great, stand before God, and the books were opened: and another book was opened, which is the book of life: and the dead were judged out of those things which were written in the books, according to their works. And the sea gave up the dead which were in it, and death and hell delivered up the dead which were in them: and they were judged every man according to their works. And death and hell were cast into the lake of fire. This is the second death. And whosoever was not found written in the book of life was cast into the lake of fire."

Revelation 21:8 also declares, "But the fearful, and unbelieving, and the abominable, and murderers, and whoremongers, and sorcerers, and idolaters, and all liars, shall have their part in the lake which burneth with fire and brimstone: which is the second death."

Into hell will the beast and the false prophet be thrown. At the end of the age, the devil himself will be thrown into it, along with death and hades and all whose names are not in the Book of Life. "And they will be tormented day and night forever and ever," according to Revelation 20:10. Because of the symbolic nature of the language, some people question whether hell consists of actual fire. Such reasoning should bring no comfort to the lost. The reality is greater than the symbolism. The Bible exhausts human language in describing and comprehending fully heaven and hell. The former is more glorious, and the latter more terrible and horrific than what a language can express.

To shed more light on the nature of this hell, sometimes, in the explanation to my children when they were younger, as we all know, at a certain growth time in life, children want to know and ask about everything they have heard or seen. So, I tried to liken hell to an angry volcanic mountain's content that is violently moving within the mountain and cannot come out to the surface of the earth. I always tell them that God reveals things to us in various ways. He allows things to happen in order to enable us to learn from those things around us. The example of something like an erupting volcanic mountain that is coming right up from deep down the earth seems, though, not a good enough comparison, but it's the closest imperfect example of what could be down there in hell. Hell content or lava is concealed or hidden as something in a prison yard; it is not flowing out, hotter than the lava from the volcanic eruption, and it is just within hell. It never dries up, never cools down, never stops flowing, and it is eternally burning the inhabitants. This portrayal, while symbolic, seeks to convey the relentless and unending nature of the torment, illustrating that the fire within hell is not merely a fleeting punishment but an eternal, unquenchable source of agony for those who find themselves separated from the divine.

Hell is an awful and horrible place of complete darkness where fire burns all the time. It is a place not to be joked with. Everywhere are worms and maggots that never die. A place where no one returns from, an abyss where there is no more mercy or grace. There is eternal wailing, weeping and gnashing of teeth. The burning hell is a complete place of torment, punishments, depression, grief, sorrow, sadness, crying, aches and pains that no one wants to see with his or her eyes. It is full of sufferings of all types, shades and forms: no food to eat, no water to drink, and no comfort of whatever sort. It is a total destruction, disastrous, frightening, scary, horrific and dreadful place of torment where there is no peace or rest of mind throughout eternity.

What Will Happen to the Wicked in Hellfire, according to the Bible?

Is there an Eternal Hell? What does the Bible say?

Will there come a day of destruction for the wicked?
Yes, for Job 21:30 says, "That the wicked is reserved to the day of destruction? They shall be brought forth to the day of wrath."

• **How will they be destroyed?** According to Psalms 21:9, "Thou shalt make them as a fiery oven in the time of thine anger: the LORD shall swallow them up in his wrath, and the fire shall devour them."

• **What will happen to evildoers?** Psalms 37:9 says, "For evildoers shall be cut off: but those that wait upon the LORD, they shall inherit the earth."

• **What will happen to the wicked?** Psalms 37:10 states, "For yet a little while, and the wicked shall not be: yea, thou shalt diligently consider his place, and it shall not be."

• **Will the wicked go on living throughout eternity?** Psalms 37:20 says, "But the wicked shall perish, and the enemies of the LORD shall be as the fat of lambs: they shall consume; into smoke shall they consume away."

• **So the wicked will be destroyed and not burn forever?** As written in Psalms 37:38, "But the transgressors shall be destroyed together: the end of the wicked shall be cut off."

• **But doesn't "cut off" only mean they will be separated from God?** "As smoke is driven away, so drive them away: as wax melteth before the fire, so let the wicked perish at the presence of God." says Psalms 68:2.

• **So then, this must mean that the wicked will be no more or consumed?** Yes, it is written in Psalms 104:35, "Let the sinners be consumed out of the earth, and let the wicked be no more. Bless thou the LORD, O my soul. Praise ye the LORD."

• **So there will be a final destruction of the wicked, they will not burn in hell for eternity?** "The LORD preserveth all them that love him: but all the wicked will he destroy," says Psalms 145:20.

• **What method will God use to destroy the wicked?** Isaiah 47:14 states, "Behold, they shall be as stubble; the fire shall burn them; they shall not deliver themselves from the power of the flame: there shall not be a coal to warm at, nor fire to sit before it."

• **But I thought the soul never dies?** Ezekiel 18:4 declares, "Behold, all souls are mine; as the soul of the father, so also the soul of the son is mine: the soul that sinneth, it shall die."

• **Will the wicked be burned up completely?** And it says in Ezekiel 28:18, "Thou hast defiled thy sanctuaries by the multitude of thine iniquities, by the iniquity of thy traffic; therefore will I bring forth a fire from the midst of thee, it shall devour thee, and I will bring thee to ashes upon the earth in the sight of all them that behold thee."

• **So, will they cease to exist?** Yes, for Ezekiel 28:19 says, "All they that know thee among the people shall be astonished at thee: thou shalt be a terror, and never shalt thou be any more."

• **How does God feel about the final destruction of the wicked?** It is written in Ezekiel 33:11, "Say unto them, as I live, saith the Lord GOD, I have no pleasure in the death of the wicked; but that the wicked turn from his way and live: turn ye, turn ye from your evil ways; for why will ye die, O house of Israel?"

• **So, after the destruction of the wicked, sin will never rise up again?** Nahum 1:9-10 asks, "What do ye imagine against the LORD? He will make an utter end: affliction shall not rise up the second time. For a while, they be folden together as thorns, and while they are drunken as drunkards, they shall be devoured as stubble fully dry."

• **How complete will the final destruction of the wicked be?** According to Malachi 4:1, "For, behold, the day cometh, that shall burn as an oven; and all the proud, yea, and all that do wickedly, shall be stubble: and the day that cometh shall burn them up, saith the LORD of hosts, that it shall leave them neither root nor branch."

• **Does the New Testament talk about the destruction of the wicked?** Yes, it is written in Matthew 7:13, "Enter ye in at the strait gate: for wide is the gate, and broad is the way, that leadeth to destruction, and many there be which go in thereat:"

• **Does the New Testament speak about the soul dying?** Yes, in Matthew 10:28 it says, "And fear not them which kill the body, but are not able to kill the soul: but rather fear him which is able to destroy both soul and body in hell."

• **When will all of this take place?** According to Matthew 13:40, "As therefore the tares are gathered and burned in the fire; so shall it be in the end of this world."

• **Matthew 25:41 speaks of "everlasting fire" for the wicked. Does it go out?** "Then shall he say also unto them on the left hand, Depart from me, ye cursed, into everlasting fire, prepared for the devil and his angels:" as per Matthew 25:41.

Yes, according to the Bible, it does. We must let the Bible explain itself. Sodom and Gomorrah were destroyed with everlasting, or eternal, fire, and that fire turned them "into ashes" as a warning to "those that after should live ungodly." "Even as Sodom and Gomorrah, and the cities about them in like manner, giving themselves over to fornication, and going after strange flesh, are set forth for an example, suffering the vengeance of eternal fire," says Jude 1:7. "And turning the cities of Sodom and Gomorrah into ashes condemned them with an overthrow, making them an example unto those that after should live ungodly;" according to 2 Peter 2:6.

These cities are not burning today. The fire went out after everything was burned up. The imagery of these cities being turned into ashes serves as a powerful warning against ungodliness. The use of the term "eternal fire" highlights the severity of divine retribution for those who turn away from righteousness.

Likewise, everlasting fire will go out after it has turned the wicked to ashes. "And ye shall tread down the wicked;

for they shall be ashes under the soles of your feet in the day that I shall do this, saith the LORD of hosts," in Malachi 4:3.

The effects of the fire are everlasting, but not the burning itself.

• **Doesn't Matthew 25:46 say the wicked will receive "everlasting punishment?"** Yes, "And these shall go away into everlasting punishment: but the righteous into life eternal," in Matthew 25:46.

Notice the word is punishment, not punishing. Punishing would be continuous, while punishment is one act. The punishment of the wicked is death, and this death is everlasting. Nowhere in Scripture will you find that the wicked will receive eternal life, only the righteous.

• **What will happen to the saved?** "For God so loved the world, that he gave his only begotten Son, that whosoever believeth in him should not perish, but have everlasting life," as written in John 3:16.

• **What are the wages of sin according to the book of Romans?** "For the wages of sin is death, but the gift of God is eternal life through Jesus Christ our Lord," says Romans 6:23.

• **What will happen to the devil? Will he also be destroyed?** Hebrews 2:14 states, "Forasmuch then as the children are partakers of flesh and blood, he also himself likewise took part of the same; that through death he might destroy him that had the power of death, that is, the devil;"

• **Why is it impossible for sinners to be in the presence of God?** "For our God is a consuming fire," says Hebrews 12:29.

• **What example does the Bible use to show that God will destroy the wicked by fire?** It says in 2 Peter 2:6, "And turning the cities of Sodom and Gomorrah into ashes condemned them with an overthrow, making them an example unto those that after should live ungodly;"

• **Where will this fire occur which destroys the wicked?** 2 Peter 3:7 writes, "But the heavens and the earth, which are now, by the same word, are kept in store, reserved unto fire against the Day of Judgment and perdition of ungodly men."

• **Doesn't God want us to repent?** Yes, He does. 2 Peter 3:9 states, "The Lord is not slack concerning his promise, as some men count slackness; but is longsuffering to us-ward, not willing that any should perish, but that all should come to repentance."

• **What will happen to the whole earth?** As written in 2 Peter 3:10, "But the day of the Lord will come as a thief in the night; in the which the heavens shall pass away with a great noise, and the elements shall melt with fervent heat, the earth also and the works that are therein shall be burned up."

• **If we miss out on the first resurrection, will we have a "second chance?"** Revelation 20:6 states, "Blessed and holy is he that hath part in the first resurrection: on such the second death hath no power, but they shall be priests of God and of Christ and shall reign with him a thousand years."

• **Where will the fire come from?** According to Revelation 20:9, "And they went up on the breadth of the earth, and compassed the camp of the saints about, and the beloved city: and fire came down from God out of heaven, and devoured them."

• **What is the second death?** It is written in Revelation 20:14, "And death and hell were cast into the lake of fire. This is the second death."

• **Are there any more verses that talk about the second death?** Yes, Revelation 21:8. It says, "But the fearful, and unbelieving, and the abominable, and murderers, and whoremongers, and sorcerers, and idolaters, and all liars, shall have their part in the lake which burneth with fire and brimstone: which is the second death."

• **What about the verse in Revelation 20:10, which talks about the devil, the beast, and the false prophet being tormented forever and ever? Doesn't that show that hellfire is forever or eternal?** Yes, Revelation 20:10, And the devil that deceived them was cast into the lake of fire and brimstone, where the beast and the false prophet are, and shall be tormented day and night forever and ever."

The term "forever," as used in the Bible, means simply a period of time, limited or unlimited.

THE CONCLUSION

"Every man's work shall be made manifest: for the day shall declare it because it shall be revealed by fire; and the fire shall try every man's work of what sort it is," according to 1 Corinthians 3:13. "But the fearful, and unbelieving, and the abominable, and murderers, and whoremongers, and sorcerers, and idolaters, and all liars, shall have their part in the lake, which burneth with fire and brimstone: which is the second death," says Revelation 21:8. "But, For God so loved the world, that He gave His only begotten Son, that whosoever believeth in Him should not perish, but have everlasting life," says John 3:16.

EVERYTHING BEGINS WITH JESUS…

An abundant life filled with love, joy, peace, happiness, patience, and victory begins with personal contact and developing a relationship with the Lord Jesus Christ. You can personally meet Jesus today by making a simple decision to receive Him and all that He has done and completed for you. He gave His life for you on the cross of Calvary so that you could be made completely free from sin, your past and all guilt and condemnation of whatever form. Because of His unconditional love, you can come right now to Him and receive Him as your Lord and Saviour; He has been waiting for you.

Pray this prayer right now and experience His life and peace in your heart for the rest of your life.

"Heavenly Father, I believe Jesus came to die for me so that I might have eternal life. It is written in Your Holy Word that if I confess with my mouth that Jesus is Lord and believe in my heart that You have raised Him from the dead, I shall be saved. Therefore, I recognise my sins, and I repent of my old ways of life. I now confess that Jesus is my Lord. I receive Him as Lord of my life right now. I believe in my heart that you raised Jesus from the dead. I renounce my past life with the Devil, and I break every covenant and all agreement with the Devil, and I close the door to any of his schemes and devices. The blood of Jesus now washes and cleanses me from all sins. I thank You for saving and making me righteous through Your grace. Jesus is now my Lord and Saviour. I am a new creation. Old things have passed away, and all things become new in Jesus Christ. Amen."

If and when you have prayed this prayer sincerely, you have been born again; you can please contact me and let me rejoice together with the Angels in Heaven who are rejoicing because of you and also to lift you up through prayer, in your commitment of faith to the Lord Jesus Christ. I beseech you to look for a Bible-believing Church where you can grow in His word.

God bless you.

Shalom!

ABOUT THE AUTHOR

Stephanie Olufunso Abraham accepted Christ at an early age and began to grow under the powerful ministry of Archbishop Benson Idahosa of the Church of God Mission. She was also mentored by Dr. I.K.U. Ibeneme (of blessed memories), the founder of the Faith Clinic, where she attended the Bible School of the Faith Clinic Inc., a deliverance ministry based in Ibadan, Nigeria, where she was born. Over the years, she has been mentored by various shepherds, according to Jeremiah 3:15, a Word received by the Lord. She realised her God-given purpose to be a Woman of worth, spreading the gospel of Jesus Christ to all through the mediums of teaching and mentoring. She is divinely called by the grace of our Lord Jesus Christ as an Apostle and a Teacher. A Warrior Princess, blessed by God to carry a mantle of honour and called to the battlefront to snatch people from hell, binding their broken hearts and setting them free from various captivities in the name of Jesus Christ and the fire of the Holy Ghosts according to Mark 3: 20-30. She operates under the powerful anointing of the Holy Spirit in the revelation and utterance of gifts. Being called by the Lord to be a repairer of the broken walls, to remove the spots and smoothen the wrinkles through the Preaching and Teaching of His Word, revealing and showing strong, hidden truths of the Word of God to "Affect, Change and encourage Full Enjoyment of Life" as in John 10:10b.

She serves at Harbour House Worldwide, Ireland, as well as the Victory Mission Abroad, a ministry designed to reach out to the world, positively changing and affecting the lives of everyone who is truly willing to be changed and be affected by the Word of God. She oversees the "Victory Family Fellowship, Drogheda, Ireland" and "Women of Vision International" which are Ministries geared to spiritually, emotionally, psychologically and physically develop wholeness in Christ. She travels by the 'Go Ye' mandate under "Apostle Stephanie Abraham Ministries" A.k.a "Living Fully Ministries," designed to procure unity and wholeness within the body of Christ through mission assignments, seminars, conferences and other corporate gatherings. She is known and loved for her wisdom, grace, honesty, integrity and sobriety. She is blessed with five children and grandchildren. She is a divine citizen of The Royal Netherlands and Europe.

www.ingramcontent.com/pod-product-compliance
Lightning Source LLC
Chambersburg PA
CBHW071203300726
48975CB00004B/1271